WHEN WORDS COLLIDE

A collection of speculative short fiction
by The Warped Spacers

Chris Crowe

Lee Garrett

Dennis Grayson

Leonard Little

Judy Prey

Stephen Prey

Amy Rogers

Caroline Williams

ISBN 9781729315965 (paperback)

FIC028040 FICTION / Science Fiction / Collections & Anthologies
FIC003000 FICTION / Anthologies (multiple authors)

The Spacers want to thank all our families and friends for their unfailing support and encouragement.

A special thanks to Jane O'Riva, Jim Czajkowski, Matt Bishop, Matt Orr, and Judy Crowe.

Also thanks to Amy Rogers for book interior design, Stephen Prey for publishing tech, Frank Barrera for cover design, and Judy Prey for nurturing the entire project from concept to completion.

Table of Contents

Paranormal

SciFi

Horror

THE TALE OF LADY MEI LAN

Judy Prey

I T WAS COLD THE day I died. The mists hung heavy on the hills and settled about us like a white robe of mourning. From the window of my palanquin, I could barely see the trees along the road. My tiny bound feet, encased in phoenix-shaped shoes, ached so in the damp. I am Lady Mei Lan, sister of the mighty Warlord Chen Shang. To complain would not be proper.

I could hear the grumbling of the soldiers as they walked beside the porters. Their padded blue tunics bearing the Chen red dragon crest hardly kept out the cold.

"Why do we go to Lord Woo's prefecture in the winter?" said a thin archer in too loud a whisper. "I heard Lord Tai offered many strings of gold for Lady Mei Lan to be his wife."

Ah, Tai Yuanming! I had loved him since we were children. However, the desires of a mere woman were of no concern to the great lords of the Yellow River valleys.

Another soldier pointed his thumb rudely at me as if I was only a mute statue. "Woo offered more gold plus three border villages. He has no sons to assure his worship as honored ancestor, only daughters. She is the only available lady of high breeding."

"What about Lord Tseng Po? He wanted her too and isn't a timid man. He'll see this trade as an affront to his position as Tenth Nephew to the Emperor."

The archer kicked a stone in the rough road. "Who are we to say? All we do is trudge for days to satisfy Lord Pig-Belly Woo's lust."

"Shh, you blind rat," said the other. "Someone might hear."

"What if they do? Lord Chen will anger all the warlords with his ambition. Mark my words. We'll be at war soon, and our wives will be wearing white before the New Year comes."

I looked through the other window as my brother rode by, then paused for the porters to come near. He had not heard the soldiers' loose talk. His face was passionless, as always. He sat straight on his sturdy mountain horse, moving as though they were one creature. His long white tabard, embroidered with clouds and birds of gold by my own hand, contrasted starkly with the shiny black coat of his mount. The gold tassel on his high, conical hat swayed with each step, mesmerizing.

Many thought my brother handsome, regal. His wives worshiped him and gave him many sons. His lackeys feared him, some said for good reason. I had always loved him. He had never been cruel to me and, sometimes, even kind.

"Sister, why do you look so sad? You mar such perfect beauty," Shang said, his smile almost mocking.

"I worry for you, brother. I heard in the women's inner chambers that Lord Tseng was very angry. I also fear Lord Tai will take offense. Father agreed I would be his. I could be happy in the home of Lord Tai."

His eyes narrowed, cold as the mist. "Don't whimper, little sister. I promise you all will be well. Plans have changed since Father's death. I do what I must."

He jerked the horse's reins sharply and rode to the head of the column. Abandoned, I fell back onto the cushions of the little box and cried in frustration at my fate.

A terrible scream halted the men. Leaning forward, I looked out the window. Something shiny caught my eye. No one lived in these dark woods. The peasants said they were haunted. Only fearless bandits camped there to lay in wait for victims foolish enough to take this shorter route through the foothills. Fear gripped my heart like a cold claw.

"Attack!" the trees seemed to shout. Out rushed swarms of men to engulf our small band. The porters dropped their burden to take up their weapons. My palanquin fell on its side, pinning me inside. I was trapped. I slid to the small, open window to watch the battle. Men fought about me with a deafening clash of iron and war cries. I watched my brother cut down two ragged-looking men with his sword. Some of our attackers wore uniforms that bore a familiar crest. One came near and I saw on his back the green hawk emblem of the Tai family.

"No," I wailed to the gods. "This can not be."

He turned and leered at me. He was scruffy and looked more brigand than soldier. A long scar dragged down a corner of his mouth exposing his black teeth. "Too bad there's no time for fun," he laughed as he plunged a spear through the window.

I felt the pain in my chest for only a few cold moments. "Where are you, brother?" I cried as I died.

~

Like a butterfly on a breeze, I floated above the carnage. There was no pain, only peace. I watched my brother's men rout the last of our attackers. My body was neatly laid out by the righted palanquin, my brother kneeling beside me. His sobs were heard by all those gathered near.

My soul was touched by Shang's outpouring of grief.

He stood slowly, turning to the north. Shaking his fist, my brother's voice echoed through the lingering mists. "You shall pay for this, Tai Yuanming! Captain, gather your men. We continue to Lord Woo's."

The old soldier paused. He could not look away from my face. A look of surprised horror distorted my delicate features, my blank eyes still staring at the clearing sky. A red rose of blood blossomed on the pale blue of my dress.

"Put her in the litter," my brother said, hastily. "I shall bury her with Woo's ancestors."

The column headed east. I floated above them for a while and then heard a sweet, familiar voice.

"Come, Mei Lan," my mother said, reaching her hand to me. "It is time to join your ancestors."

She floated beside me, bathed in shimmering light. Her smile filled me with longing to be with the spirits of my family. I took her hand and turned my head toward a wondrous radiance. Before I could draw too near, I stopped, trembling in a sudden rage. Mother released my hand, looking at me quizzically.

"I cannot go, Mother. I must know why I was murdered. I cannot rest till then."

"Beware child," she said with a sad smile. "The demon dogs feast on the souls of those with anger and hatred in their hearts. Come to us when you have found your answers."

As an invisible wraith, I looked down from the roof of Woo Fang's open temple. It nestled in a far corner of the large walled compound. My brother and Woo Fang knelt before a golden statue of Lord Buddha. The great lords wore the plain clothes of mourners. My body, also draped in white, lay on a bier beside them. Woo sobbed loudly, clapped his hands three times to wake the gods to hear the prayers. They lit joss paper in the altar fire. A saffron-robed priest rang a small bell to alert my spirit that the proper offerings were coming up to heaven for me to enjoy. Beside the fire lay a tray of rare fruits and small jade baubles. The priest chanted as Woo heaved onto his skinny legs. He and my brother bowed three times and left the small family temple, the mournful sound of the chant following them.

I drifted behind them as they walked towards the main house on the other side of the large garden. Lord Woo was rightly proud of his "Heavenly Oasis." Carefully trimmed fruit trees, graceful in their winter's nakedness, in the spring brought forth fragrances and colors fit to delight the gods.

My brother paused beside a bench carved in the shape of a crouching tiger. "Woo Fang, you must answer me. We must not let Tai think he has stricken us with his cowardly blow. We must act swiftly."

Woo looked up at my brother. I saw genuine tears on his pudgy little face. "Chen Shang," he said, dropping wearily to the bench. "I understand your righteous indignation. Your sister, almost the mother of my sons, has been killed. It might have been by a man we all called neighbor and friend. It might also have been Lord Tseng or even bandits in tunics stolen from dead soldiers. You are a warrior, as was your father. The four warlords of the Yellow River valleys carved out their prefectures during the chaos after the fall of Emperor Tang." He paused, looking up. I worried that he might see me. I wasn't used to being a ghost yet. " We also benefit from the peace they agreed upon. I do not wish to rush into a war that could destroy us without consulting my generals and astrologers. Besides, planning a war is improper during our period of grief. Come, my friend, it is time for the mourning feast. My cook makes the best roast goose in all the valleys. And his Thousand Year Eggs are fit for the Emperor."

The thought of food gave the heavy man a lightness of step as he led my brother into his house.

I floated down to sit on the crouching tiger and looked into its upturned face. It had the eyes of my brother and said in its silent way, "Be strong."

That night I came to my brother's bedroom. He sat on a high platform bed, its heavy curtains drawn aside. Leaning before an oil lamp, he studied a detailed map of the four prefectures. Running his finger along our northern border, he paused at a high pass. Tapping it, he smiled. His eyes held a glazed resolve I had never seen before.

I called his name. He looked up, quickly rolling the bamboo parchment and slipped it into a leather container. He jumped off the bed to search the room.

"Hah," he said, tugging at the neck of his robe. "Must have been that goose."

He turned to climb into the bed, pulling the curtains closed. He settled under the warm covers and was soon snoring, then mumbling in a dream.

I willed myself to enter his dream. I saw my brother standing in his wives' quarters, kissing a naked woman. He stepped back to admire her delicate form. I realized it was Chia No, Tai's youngest sister. He fondled her breasts and grunted in his lust.

I stepped forward, robed in the clothes of my death. Blood stained the delicate blue, and gore dripped from the open wound in my chest. "Shang," I called again. "You promised my safety. My spirit cannot rise to heaven until I know why I died. You must seek my murderer."

Fear, then horror, then anger crossed his face. "Be gone, ghost," he yelled. "You were only a woman. We were attacked. You were killed. I say enough of this."

The force of his emotion expelled me from the dream. I retreated to the sanctuary of the temple to think. Why was my brother angry with me? Or was he ashamed of his grief for a sister?

∽

The next day I appeared before Lord Woo's four learned astrologers as a direful wraith. They sat beside a garden pond, luxuriating in the unseasonably warm sun. I moaned and cried woe for an untimely death. I waved my arms and pointed to the great, gaping hole in my chest. They were quite aghast at the sight. One dropped his star maps, falling out of his chair in a dead faint. His young apprentice doused the old man with a large mug of wine. It woke him but did not improve his mood.

"How can you plan for war?" I wailed. "This is only the first moon, not the time of year to contemplate the taking of life. The gods will be offended. Terrible calamities will befall your sons and bad luck will follow all of your descendants."

They all shrieked in horror, running from the garden and then pushing at each other to leave the front gate first. Lord Woo and my brother, drawn to the courtyard by their screams, confronted the last and slowest one.

"Lords," said the astrologer, his knees knocking louder than thunder. "We have conferred and predict disaster. We advise you to desist from your plans for war. I must leave. My condolences, Lord Chen. We'll send you our bill, Lord Woo." He bowed very low and raced out the gate.

My brother riveted the smaller man with a cold look. "They speak nonsense. I shall consult my own astrologers. After the burial tomorrow, I shall return home. My runners will contact you when a plan is made."

Woo opened then closed his mouth. He quietly followed the determined strides of my brother into the house.

I feared I had won only a short delay before my brother shattered the peace of the River Valleys. I still knew nothing of why I had been murdered. I felt the kindness in my soul grow colder than a winter frost. It was replaced by an anger as black as a moonless night. It was then I first saw the burning red eyes leering at me from around the gate. I quickly averted my gaze. Were these the devil dogs hungering for my soul?

Many days later I watched as my brother broke the news of the terrible event to a meeting of his generals and vassals. I peered through an open window of the large main room. My brother's priests had placed ghost wards about the house so I could not enter. The men wore their best embroidered robes. The flags of the vassal families rustled lightly in the breeze from the window. This was an important day. Shang spoke of treachery, my chaste beauty, Woo's anguish at the loss of future sons. He swore revenge against Lord Tai, throwing down a bloody tunic with a green hawk emblem at their feet.

Oh, how I wanted to appear before them, but I could not materialize. I watched as they all roared for revenge.

I wanted justice, not the slaughter of great armies. But, how could I stop it? Lord Chen stood firm in his cold purpose. He would not heed his ghostly sister or learned astrologers. What could I do?

I floated up to the clouds of heaven to consult my father and the other ancestors who abide there.

"Child, the force of your emotion surprises me," father said. We stood in a great hall not unlike our earthly home but on a grander scale. The walls here were covered with paintings of dragons and the gods. "Heed my words daughter. Beware that anger does not consume you. Call on your ancestors or the Goddess of Mercy when you need our help."

I lowered my head to honor my father and to hide my tears of frustration. Even as a child, when it was not seemly to direct my anger at its proper target, I would cry. How delicate and feminine they all thought. How constrained as a right-thinking female I felt.

Time has no meaning to a spirit. I did not realize that while I was in the heavenly clouds, it had become spring. Returning to my brother's household, I found it buzzing like an overturned hive. While I was gone, Shang had joined his army with Lord Woo's and, despite Lord Tai's protestations of innocence, was about to face him on the plains below the Crescent Moon Hills.

I could not let this be, so I raced on the wind. In the drop of a tear I hovered above the hills. Lord Tseng's armies lay hidden in the nearby valley, awaiting the outcome so that his army could swoop down on the winner, weakened by days of battle. The slights to his name and his pride were enough reason for him to wage war. Yet, could Tseng have been my murderer? Was this all a plot to prove he was worthy to join his uncle at the imperial court? I did not think he was clever enough to plan such a coup.

I watched the two great armies advance. My brother held the advantage of the higher ground and the combined strength of two prefectures. The soldiers in their blue and yellow tunics fluttered down from the high hills like strange, sinister butterflies. The lines of their long ranks seemed end-less. Shang rode before them.

Farther down the hill, Lord Tai sat on his prancing white horse proud and determined. He was no coward and would fight to the death. I could not have Yuanming in life, but I did not want his death. So many men would die this day.

My rage rose in me, almost consuming me, yet giving me raw power. I drew the clouds about me. Thrusting them over the hills and plain, they darkened, infected with my rage. The armies below were pelted with black hail. Mighty crashes of thunder and blinding bolts of lightning cowed even the bravest of the warriors. They huddled against each other waiting for the unearthly storm to pass.

I cleared a small break in the clouds, floating down to where my brother had drawn rein. I appeared before them in all my terrible ghostly wonder. My blue robe bore the Chen crest of the red dragon. On my feet were tiny shoes made of phoenix feathers. I transfixed every man with my burning stare. Even my brother blanched. The dragon was only to be worn by the males of my family.

I moaned and pointed about me. "Who is responsible for the death of Chen Mei Lan? I shall not rest until I know. Who?" The sound echoed down the hills, through all the valleys, drumming the question into the hearts of the men below. They looked at one another hoping someone would confess and put an end to my rage.

A far away unearthly howling blended with the final note of the echo, emphasizing my anguish.

My brother nudged his skittish horse to the top of a small rise where he could be easily seen. "Little sister, you waste your efforts. They avail you nothing. I am determined to avenge your death. These priests will send you back to the heavens where you belong." He quietly sat there as his priests gathered about him and began a low, rumbling chant.

I could feel my power ebbing. With my last bit of will, I called upon the spirits of the heavens to give me strength.

All became very still. Even the howling ceased. The clouds thinned, then spit forth a host of nine dragons breathing icy mist.. On their backs sat the spirits of nine great warlords, my father at the fore. His great red dragon swooped down and snared first Lord Tseng, then the other three warlords in his mighty claw. He settled on a nearby low hill, opening his fist so all the men could see the lords. The other beasts and their riders hovered over the battlefield like undulating yellow, green, and black kites.

"It is time to speak the truth." My father's soft voice thundered through the hills. "Who breaks the peace of the River Valleys? Who murdered my child?"

The following silence was deafening. Even the wind gods held their breath. The four men looked at one another and then at the dragons, awed by the precariousness of their predicament.

The smell of fear and anger drew the demon dogs onto the battleground inspite ot their inate fear of the dragons. They were hungry for the souls of those who had strayed from the right path. Their ebon hides cast no shadow, and to look into their fiery eyes meant madness. The demons ran to the great dragon, leaping and howling at the quaking mortals standing in the claw.

Father turned his icy gaze to Lord Woo.

"Oh no, Great Lord. You cannot think it was me. Why would I kill the future mother of my sons?" He fell to his knees, his hands clasped tightly under his trembling chin. "My line shall die with me. There will be no sons to say the proper prayers at my funeral. My ghost shall wander without a home." A tear rolled down his full cheek to splash on a claw with a silvery tinkle.

"No, Woo," my father said. "You may be weak, but in your heart you are a good man. You should pay more attention to your current two wives."

Lord Woo's obvious joy seemed to disappoint the seething black pack on the ground.

"And you, Tai, the son of my old friend. What is your answer to my child's question?"

Tai simply turned toward me. "I have loved Mei Lan since we were young. I would sooner cut off my arm than harm her."

The pack whimpered in pain as the warmth of our love wafted down to them.

I felt my rage ebb slowly from my soul like a breeze blowing out a candle.

Straightening his back, Lord Tseng turned to glare boldly at Father. He thumped his chest. "As Tenth Nephew of the Great Emperor, I have no need to murder an insignificant female. "

The demon dogs leaped higher. The taste of arrogance was even more savory than fear or anger. My father smiled at the little man as if to say that Tseng would face his judgment soon enough.

Then, as if we all were one giant creature, we turned our eyes to the one remaining man who stood defiantly in the dragon's claw.

"Yes, Father. I did it for our family honor," said my brother, stepping away from the others. "My meek little sister, who would have thought you capable of such a rage. You were merely a small sacrifice in my plan. Your murder was the rally cry to gather these armies. With victory here, I can march from the North valleys to the very walls of Kaifeng. Can't you see me dressed in Imperial yellow robes, beginning the glorious Chen dynasty? It is my destiny."

His maniacal laughter rolled down the hills, mixing with my shrieks of pain and outrage. It washed over the stunned armies. In their frenzy, the demon beasts jumped to the level of the claw.

The dogs below me snapped their fangs and leapt in the air. My chaotic emotions were tasty morsels dangling over their slavering jaws.

My father and his great mount shuddered at the hideous tale of betrayal and greed. My brother lost his balance, and fell to the ground screaming.

The dogs circled him, their sharp fangs dripping steaming saliva. They crowded close, savoring the delicious fear of their victim. They nipped at him, then danced in to rake his silk robe.

"Forgive me, sister," he cried, true tears of sorrow falling from his dark eyes. "I have wronged you terribly. The desire to be emperor drove me to destroy us all."

I looked down into the fiery eyes of two devil dogs.

So near!

They could only have been drawn by my lingering anger. This realization and my brother's tears shook me. To forgive my brother, I had to let go of my rage. Yuanming's love was not enough to protect me.

"Kuan Yin," I cried. "Goddess of Mercy save us from the evil we have wrought."

A beautiful maiden suddenly appeared on a golden cloud. She reached down to pluck my brother's soul from the jaws of the largest dog. They all fled, returning to their lair to await the next meal of foolish mortal. Each dangled a piece of Shang's mangled body from bloody jaws.

Kuan Yin turned toward the awaiting spirits, releasing my brother's ghost to us.

"Go now. Be at peace." Her smile filled us with wonder and comfort. She vanished in a ripple of sweet song.

My soul felt whole again.

Kneeling before our father, Shang no longer looked crazed, only humble. Father leaned forward to beckon my brother to sit behind him on the dragon.

The dragons and their riders cleared from the sky, ascending to their homes in the heavens.

The remaining lords began the long trek to their valley homes, vowing to remember the words of the Goddess. The armies' fears melted like hail in the sunlight.

I floated down to Yuanming's side. My ghostly hand wiped away a tear as it fell slowly down his cheek. We both vowed that someday our spirits would be together, never to be parted.

SHANE

Leonard Little

I SAT STARING OUT THE passenger side window as my social worker from Children's Services, Mrs. Rodriguez, stopped the van in front of a two-story brick house. It was the last in a long line of foster parents that were willing to take this half-wild Indian boy with no ties to the past and no future.

"Wait here while I go in and talk with Mr. and Mrs. Stone," she said.

I looked away as she got out. Staring into the side mirror, I lost myself in the reflection. Anger seethed through me. I felt as if I were lost in a world that had turned its back on me.

Oh, I tried to fit in with the other kids at first, and I stayed with the first foster family that had taken me in until I was eight. That's when the foster mother I knew as Grandma, suffered a massive stroke and I was carted off without a word or a visit to the hospital to see how she had fared.

The next family only wanted the money they got for taking me in. I escaped from there at ten and lived up in the hills above Oroville for three months before a park ranger found me half-starved and freezing to death. He brought me back to the county facility and I stayed there a year before I was placed in another home.

I heard the door open and watched as Mrs. Rodriguez went inside, so I turned back to the passenger-side-mirror.

The sleeveless T-shirt I was wearing revealed the wolf tattoo on my right shoulder. I had gotten it when I was fourteen. I'd seen the picture among many as I passed the tattoo parlor and I just had to have it, so I swiped the fifty bucks I needed out of Mr. Reiley's wallet. Needless to say, I went back to the county, spending six months in Juvie for theft.

The front door of the house opened. A man followed Mrs. Rodriguez, towering over her. He was at least six-four, maybe taller. He had dark hair and high cheekbones like my own. His skin was paler than mine, but it remained the golden color of fine oak.

A sudden hope rose from the pit of my stomach that maybe this man might understand what it was like to be me, but I pushed the feeling down, knowing that things never worked out the way you wanted. I had to stay strong. Hope was knife to the guts when it failed. I was better off keeping to myself. A lone wolf howling at the moon.

A small slip of a woman with long ebony hair and dark-walnut colored skin followed Mrs. Rodriguez, who stopped half-way down the walk and called out to me. "Shane, come over here and meet your new foster parents."

I turned my head away, trying to show a lack of interest I didn't really feel.

"Listen, young man, these people are your last chance. Either you get out of that van and mind your manners, or I'll take you back right now!"

I shrugged my shoulders as if I didn't care and a part of me didn't. I couldn't afford to care. If you care about things too much, you get hurt.

I got out and met the three adults at the arched entrance to their gated front yard.

"Mr. and Mrs. Stone, this is Shane."

I kept my head down as a hand reached out to me, and I took it limply, still not wanting to show any of my hidden feelings. Mr. Stone's grip was firm and strong, but there was more to it than that. His touch set off something inside me. It was a feeling I had never felt before—a sense of belonging, like a lone wolf joining up with a neighboring pack.

"I'm John and this is Sarah."

I lifted my gaze to meet the man's eyes, seeing a sliver of gold behind his brown contact lenses.

My eyes were deep blue when I was younger, but they faded to light green and were now showing a yellowish tint around the edges. I wondered if John could possibly be a lost uncle or second cousin?

He smiled, his sharp canine teeth showing at the edges of his grin. "I think the boy will feel right at home with us, Mrs. Rodriguez. Thank you for bringing him to us."

"It's people like you who should be thanked. Not many couples will take in a troubled teen."

"Well, I'm not proud of it, but I remember when I was a troubled teen and someone gave me a chance. I'm just returning the favor."

I stood stiff as a board in the yard and watched as Mrs. Rodriguez drove away, leaving me with a new set of strangers.

Dropping my shoulders, I let the tension trickle out of me like melting snow, knowing I was better able to survive on my own than the first time I ran away.

John's voice broke the awkward silence that followed. "I guess I'd better show you to your room, young man, so you can get yourself settled. We'll go over the rules and whatnot after dinner."

I followed John through the double doors of dark oak with long gold-edged glass panes on the top half. Inside, hardwood floors led to the plush green carpet that covered the living room and ran up the stairway to the top floor. It was the finest house I had ever been in. Everything was neat and clean. The last place I lived in was anything but clean, except when Social Services was due to visit.

John climbed the stairs and opened the second door on the right. "This used to be my room a while back. I think the clothes should fit you as well, but if they don't, we'll take you into town tomorrow for anything you need."

I waited in silence until John left, closing the door behind him.

He cracked the door back open and said, "I'll come get you for dinner at six."

I listened to his footsteps until they faded into the carpeted stairs before I went to the closet to see what kind of lame hand-me-downs I'd have to wear this time.

The crap I found went beyond lame. This was the kind of stuff you'd wear if you wanted to end up face down in the toilet with piss swirling around your head. Checkered slacks and plaid shirts with matching jackets, all nearly new and hanging neatly beside the only cool thing there. A black leather jacket with the skull of a wolf embroidered in silver on the back, hung off to one side like even it knew it didn't belong with the other clothes.

I put it on thinking the sleeves would have to go, but I'd learned enough leathercraft in the county home to do the job.

Silver studs at neck and shoulders ought to finish it off quite well.

I spent the rest of the afternoon wondering how John could have worn these things when he was my age.

The knock for dinner came straight up at six, and I headed downstairs still wearing the leather jacket.

John smiled as I sat at the table. "I see you found something you could wear."

I looked him straight in the eye and said, "Nothing else fit." The gold of Mr. Stone's eyes flared, stopping the lie still on my tongue. I tried again, but the words slid away as I tried to speak.

Sarah broke our eye contact as she set a steaming platter of pot roast between me and John.

Fear ripped through my center like a swollen river cutting a narrow bank. I wanted to get up and run, but instincts buried deep inside told me if I ran, I would be hunted and killed just like any other prey. I stayed seated while Sarah brought in the rest of the meal and sat at her husband's right. John carved the roast giving the smallest slice to me.

I didn't eat. At least not at first, but one look from him had me wolfing the meat down in one bite.

"Good boy. Now I think it's time we show you why we were so happy when we found you." John stood up. The gold in his eyes flared again. His nose lengthened. Teeth filled his mouth. Black fur pierced through his skin covering every inch.

A lump grew in my throat. I couldn't tear my eyes away as John shook head to tail, letting his clothing fall to the floor. He turned his muzzle to Sarah and growled. Her body lengthened as it thinned. The skin below her dress mottled with scales, legs melting together forming a diamond shaped pattern that ended in a rattle. Her face flattened, hair retreated below scales covering her wedge-shaped head.

She slithered out of her dress and coiled up beside the great wolf.

John turned his golden gaze back to me and growled.

I fell out of my chair and scrambled to the back wall, but I couldn't turn away from Johns golden stare.

He lowered on his haunches and lunged at me, teeth bared, clinching around my throat.

My mouth went dry. Heart pounding in my chest, I felt a warm trickle down my legs as I shoved against his weight, trying to get away.

His huge paws pined my shoulders to the floor. Hot breath burned around my neck. I knew then, I was going to die and there was nothing I could do.

My body went limp and darkness closed in around me.

I awoke, heart still pounding in my chest. Looking up, I saw the moon and stars.

I'm outside?

I tried to get up, but something was wrong with my legs. They didn't bend right, and I only managed to get to my hands and…

Where the hell are my knees?

My toenails dug into the fabric of my tennis shoes, trying to find traction on the loose-fitting leather sole. I pushed off, trying once again to stand, but only managed to lift my body a foot before I fell back to my paws.

Paws?

Moonlight glistened over the dark fur, covering my whole body. The scream in my throat came out as high-pitched howl that ended in a whimper.

John was there, his stance indicating he'd chase me down if I ran. I shook myself, leaving my clothing in a jumbled pile as instincts warned me to crawl closer to the larger wolf.

His golden eyes met mine, opening a door in my mind.

I smell a rabbit. Hunt with me, Shane, and then I will answer your questions.

But…

A warning growl silenced me, then.

Set your mind to learning your new form. Now follow me and keep your mind open. I will show you what it means to be a wolf.

John turned his tail to me and took off. I followed, holding to the link we shared. I felt his muscles bunch and thrust and my body mimicked his. There were no words in this instruction. It was like our minds had become one. When he sniffed the air, I caught a thousand scents and more, letting his mind form pictures for each one.

One scent singled itself out from the others as we gained speed, nearly flying across an open meadow. I no longer followed in John's footsteps, but rather off to the side, as we angled inward to corner and kill our prey.

Closing in, we halted, lowering to our bellies on either side as we edged out from the cover of the trees. Again, no words were spoken, but I knew what was expected.

I saw in his mind's eye as John crept into place, blocking the entrance to the rabbit's warren.

Then I leapt from behind the tree, barking and snapping as I chased the rabbit toward John.

He sprang up and snatched the frightened creature mid-stride, shaking it between his teeth until it hung like a rag doll from his bloody mouth.

I sat back on my haunches, my stomach growling as John ripped open the soft belly with his teeth and sank his muzzle into the warm blood.

Holding the carcass with his front paws, he tore out a chunk of dark red meat and wolfed it down.

My tongue slipped out between my teeth, dampening my nose and lips as I waited for John to finish. My stomach growled again, bringing a whine to my throat. John stepped back a pace and I darted forward, burying my face in the flesh of the fat rabbit. Its warm blood tasted both salty and sweet as I bit down, tearing meat from the bones. I couldn't remember tasting anything quite so good. The soft chewy flesh slid down my throat and I ripped away more, leaving only a mat of bloody fur and bones.

I sensed that John was ready to run. He sprang into motion following the creek south out of the woods, bounding over split-rail fences or crawling under barbed wire.

We climbed the lower hills of the Buttes and crossed over to the inner circle of the range. We ran on, surrounded on all sides by the hills as if we were in the caldera of an ancient volcano.

Then John turned toward the tallest of the peaks to a near vertical rock-face.

Spirit Mountain.

What are we doing here? I asked.

To answer your questions.

I lowered onto my belly, resting my head on my paws.

We are an ancient race, older than the humans from whom we now take our first form. We came here through a portal that lies behind this wall of stone.

We're aliens? I asked.

We've been called Skinwalkers by some and Were Beasts by other cultures. Both names suggest dark magic and evil.

You mean I'm a werewolf? I'm not going to go crazy and kill everyone, am I?

Hollywood has made that name a curse, I prefer our true name, Antawa. Whether we are good, or evil is up to each individual, as in all sentient life. We take on the form of earth's animals, and then only two forms. Our second form is wolf. Sarah, however comes from the Snake Clan. Others have taken the panther or mountain lion from this area, and I have heard of monkeys and eagles in other parts of the world.

I lifted my muzzle into the air turning to gaze at the silvery disc overhead. *So, what's with the full moon?*

Earth is not our first home. For thousands of years, the moon was our home. It was different then—a twin to the earth with water and creatures of its own.

I lifted my muzzle toward the moon, sensing a longing for something lost ages ago. Before I knew it, a song broke from my throat. It echoed into the higher registers that I couldn't have heard in my human form. John joined in adding his lower timbre, which gave the song a richness I felt from nose to tail. Other wolves echoed our song, adding their tones. As the song grew, I realized I had found more than my second form that night. I had found peace and belonging. The song filled my soul, and in it I found a home, a family, a pack. I wasn't a lone wolf any more, and I would never refer to wolf-song as "howling at the moon" again.

Roxy

Chris Crowe

I DIDN'T BELIEVE IN GHOSTS until after I became one. I didn't expect to die on that particular day, but I did expect heaven, hell, or nothing, not this in-between.

I died on a rain-drenched night on an isolated portion of Highway 1, just south of Fort Bragg. I was going down to the research station at Albion to visit a friend stationed there when a big rig lost control on a tight curve. The trailer wheel smacked my brand new Vespa GTS 300 Super Scooter and sent me over the guard rail of the Little River Bridge. The last I saw of the big rig was tail-lights as I dropped toward the rocks below.

I prayed on the way down and watched the slide show of my life, but after "Now I lay me down to sleep" and a replay of 19 uneventful years, I had plenty of time to enjoy the ride.

I was rather smitten with the waves smashing against the rocks until I joined them. All hell broke loose after that: the scooter crumbled, the gas tank broke, sparks ignited the fuel, a flash of white gray light washed over me, and my body tumbled into the surf. I suppose I was already dead. The flames didn't hurt.

You've heard of those people who hover around the hospital bed while doctors and nurses frantically try to bring life back into their bodies. Well, I did hover around a bit, but when the waves and rocks had worked over what was left after the crash and the flames, there wasn't much to go back to.

I wondered if anyone had seen me go over the guard-rail and looked up to the highway hoping to see someone peering into the darkness. In a moment, I was at the edge of the road. I glanced down at the wreckage and laughed. The taillight shown bright red and the turn signal blinked left. The thought, "Left for Hell, right for Heaven," tamped my laughter to a giggle. The scooter could go where-ever it wanted. I was still on Highway 1.

The downpour reduced to a drizzle that danced through my shoulders and illuminated my form. I noticed the bangles on my wrists and sandals on my feet. I didn't ride in sandals and hadn't worn bangles for years, but they went well with the pastel blue tank top and white short-shorts that buttoned up the sides. I was 19 in my second year of college when I went over the side, but looked a lot younger. It may have been the outfit. It was odd that I knew what I looked like without a mirror. Could have been a reflection off the rain slick street or just some feature of a near death experience. Yeah, I was near death, just the other side.

Thinking I was all alone, I stepped into the middle of the road and watched an approaching truck.

"Unless you want that truck driver to join us," a voice called to me, "I suggest you get out of the road."

I looked around and saw a slender young man with a scraggly goatee, a scruffy daypack, and a Fender 12-string beckoning to me from the guardrail.

"Chester," he said as he extended a well manicured hand.

"Roxy," I said and reached to shake his hand. I noticed the Minnie Mouse watch, the one I got at Disneyland, the year I was 10, on my wrist when I reached out to shake his hand. I didn't hear his next words as I pondered the strength and warmth of his grip. Nothing cold and ghostly about it. When I realized he was talking I asked, "What did you say?"

"Are you a southpaw, a lefty?" Chester said. "Your watch."

I looked at Minnie on my right wrist and the bangles on my left and said, "No, I'm ambidextrous. I write just as poorly left-handed as I do right." I waited a moment for a reaction to one of my favorite lines and continued, "I can throw a mean curve with either hand as well. Came in handy when I pitched against the College of the Siskiyous last season."

Chester's puzzled look made me think I'd given him too much information.

"What team do you play for?" Chester asked.

"I play for Humboldt State," I stated proudly, but I could read the doubt in his eyes. I looked over the guardrail and said, "I guess that would be played under the present circumstances." The doubt deepened.

"You don't look like you're out of grade school," Chester said, "but strange things sometimes happen in the crossover."

It must be the outfit I thought as I reevaluated my looks. That odd ability to know what I looked like without a mirror came in handy for that purpose. On closer inspection, I

noticed the absence of two prominent points of my identity;
the Mansfield's were missing. I wasn't that big busted but I
was the first in my class to develop. A television documentary
on Jane's life aired about that time and the moniker stuck.
"Twelve?" I offered a hopeful guess at the age I looked.

"Closer to ten," Chester suggested.

"Humph," I vocalized. I looked at my watch and Minnie's
hands moved to 10 o'clock and while I was thinking that was
weird, she winked at me. I started to say, "Well, ten it is," but
was interrupted by an elderly couple arguing as they walked
towards us.

"If you had listened to me and stayed at the hotel," the
woman said.

"If you would have gotten ready quicker, we could have
been on the road earlier," the man said.

"That's Raymond and Silvia," Chester said. "We call them
'the keeping up with the Jones.' They drove their BMW over
the cliff back in 1969. Up here to buy investment property,
they were in a hurry to get back to civilization and left Fort
Bragg on a foggy night."

"They're old enough to be AARP's in a Winnebago," I
observed.

"They were in their 30's when they crossed over," Chester
said.

"If you had listened to me when I told you to slow down,"
Silvia said.

"If you had just shut up and let me concentrate on the road," Raymond said.

I stared as they faded into the mist. I thought my mind must have been scrambled in the fall. 'Crossed over?'

Chester got my attention, "You'll hear bits and pieces of the story each time they walk by."

A lone figure trudged up the graveled edge of the road. He had his collar turned up and face down as he approached the guardrail and peered over. He shook his head in denial.

"Who's that?" I asked.

"Not one of us," Chester said. "Let's check him out."

In a blink Chester disappeared and reappeared standing next to the man. After a few moments, Chester motioned to me and called out, "Hey, Roxy, you've gotta hear this."

I thought to take a step toward Chester and I was there.

"He's the truck driver," Chester said.

Talking to himself, the trucker said, "I know this is the place. I know something went over the edge right about here."

"Nice of you to care," I said without sarcasm. The trucker didn't hear. He just kept talking to himself. I looked out to the ocean and could not see the lights and said, "It's a little further down the road."

He seemed to hear that or just then decided to keep looking.

"Where is here, anyways?" I asked Chester.

"Casper," Chester said.

"You're kidding."

"Yeah, Casper is just down the road a piece, but it's fun to watch the newly arrived when the old ones say, 'Casper.'"

A county sheriff patrol car pulled up with its lights flashing. The deputy sheriff got out and approached the driver, "See anything?"

"Down there," the trucker pointed, "faint red lights, like tail and blinker lights."

The deputy pulled a small flashlight off her belt. Before she could turn it on, the trucker scoffed, "A flashlight?"

A flick of the switch and a powerful beam illuminated the wreckage below. "Military grade," the deputy said. "Got it on Amazon." A moment later the light skimmed across my body.

"Whoa," Me and the trucker said.

He turned away.

I stared.

"It will have to wait for the fire department," the sheriff said. "We can't get down there safely."

"So now I'm an 'it'," I said.

"I don't think she meant it like that," Chester said.

"Yeah, but she should watch how she talks in front of..." I hesitated.

"Dead people," Chester finished my thought.

"Yeah, dead people," I agreed.

A soft breeze sighed through the trees, raindrops patted on the ground, and the whine of a big-rig climbing the grade a mile away, filled the silence as conversation stopped.

Radio chatter from the deputy's car shattered the sounds of silence, and Chester said, "Our situation takes some getting used to."

I moved over to stand shoulder to shoulder with the deputy and joined her in peering into the surf below. As the light played around the scene below, the wreckage of my scooter morphed into a 49 Ford, four-door sedan. The sedan morphed into a 62 ragtop Impala, then into an old dodge Forest Service pickup, and into a 54 Woody, complete with long boards sticking out the end.

"That was mine," Chester said proudly. "Got it from my old man, a long-boarder from way back in the day. I was headed for the Mavericks in 04 after getting in some cold-water practice up this way. Went over the edge about where we're standing. I think 'one for the road' did me in."

The Woody transformed into a Beamer. "That's the 'Keeping up with the Jones,'" Chester said. And then a covered wagon appeared complete with four yoke of oxen. I giggled and Chester laughed at my reaction.

My 2014 GTS Vespa 300 Super in bright red with matching Top Case and full Chrome Trim package showed up next. I noticed that my matching helmet failed to join in the assembly and lay still and shattered bracketing my very dead head.

A 1927 Diamond Rio concrete truck with the logo, 'Find a need and Fill it' appeared next.

"I haven't figured out what that is," Chester said. "Can't quite make out the emblem."

"It's a 1927 REO Speed Wagon," I said confidently.

"Doesn't look like a bunch of long-haired, old white guys to me," Chester said doubtfully.

"Not the band, the truck they're named after," I said.

"What does a ten-year-old kid know about vintage trucks?" Chester asked.

I knew he was kidding me but I answered anyway, "My dad liked to restore old trucks. He has a '27 REO flat bed he makes into a float for the 4th of July parade every year. But what does all this mean?"

"I saw this four times before I caught on," Chester said. "It happens every time the rest gather to welcome a newcomer."

"The rest?" I questioned.

Chester turned and swept his arm in a wide arc along the hillside above the highway. My gaze followed his arm and dozens of half formed glimmers sparkled in the trees and scrubs. Singly, or in twos and threes, they took on form and substance. A kind smile or hand raised in welcome greeted me everywhere I looked. Even the 'Keeping up with the Jones's' stopped their bickering long enough to wave and smile.

"This is real?" I said more in question than fact.

"As real as it gets," Chester stated.

Ghosts of every description formed a reception line to welcome me into . . . into whatever we were, and they were friendly. They worked their way past me with smiles, handshakes, hugs, and words of welcome.

"Come visit us in Louisiana, we have a nice ante-bellum plantation on Cado Lake just outside Shreveport," a southern belle in hooped skirts encouraged me.

"When you're done with swamps, gators, and skeeters, come visit us at our castle in Scotland," a Scottish Highlander with a broadsword taller than me gave his invitation with a flourish and a bow.

I had to ask, "How did a Scottish Highlander end up on the California coast?"

He laughed. "My ship, trading between Fort Ross and the Aleutians, ran aground on the rocks below."

He pointed and I looked to see a three masted sloop in place of the '27 Reo. Just then my Vespa GTS 300 Super Scooter morphed into view.

He laughed again. "It wouldn't be a guess to say you didn't look like a ten-year-old on a Summer's day when you went over."

I didn't have time to wrap my thoughts around that, before a well accessorized 'tween stepped up. She said, "When you've had enough of moors and moss, come hangout with me at the Mall of America. Food, fun, and frolic 24/7."

When the reception line faded into the ether, I said, "From K-2 to Death Valley, from Times Square to Yellowstone, from Barrow, Alaska to Patagonia, I think I've been invited to every possible point on the planet. What do I do first?"

"Anything of interest?" Chester asked.

"That kid from Mall of America, is about my age." After a moment, I asked, "What did you do first?"

He didn't answer right away. Then, in a far-away voice, he said, "I spent a lot of time haunting my parents."

"Haunting?" I asked, thinking that was a bad thing.

"Well, we'd just call it hanging out, but those on the other side would call it haunting. My mother knew when I was around and would fill me in on all the family gossip. Dad thought it creepy the way she talked to me. But I could sense the peace when I hung out with him in the garage."

"Haunting a garage?" I smirked. "The cars must have been terrified."

"When I was a kid, he'd tinker on something Saturday mornings and listen to the Yankees on his dad's old radio. After I crossed over I'd find him out there fussing and cussing over something. I'd sit on his old army footlocker where I sat as a kid and he'd pause, look around, and relax. After he retired, we spent a lot of time together in the garage."

Chester stopped talking. He'd been happy telling about his mom and dad, but now had a serious, sad expression. I didn't know what to say. I looked out over the ocean and waited.

Chester followed my gaze to the pounding surf, and said, "I was there when Dad crossed over. Heart attack: first, fast, fatal. One moment he was gasping and clutching his chest and the next he was hugging me."

"Wow! Where is he now?" I asked and looked around expecting to see him.

"Gone. The angels took him. They came in on a beam of light, took Dad by the hand, and blinked out."

He hesitated and his expression faded from pleasant to perplexed. "The garage burst with light and filled with a host of angels. Dad reached out to them and they took him. I shouted, 'Hey, what about me?' One of the angels reached out his hand and asked, 'Are you ready?' I didn't take it. Guess I wasn't." Chester stopped talking and looked out to sea.

I didn't try to fill the silence. I tried to wrap my thoughts around 'Are you ready' wondering if that applied to me as well. The darkness fought the searchlights as firefighters and wrecking crew squabbled over who had first dibs. The wrecking crew got positively religious over damage to the environment. Something about starfish breeding season won the argument. They hoisted the remains of my Vespa out first.

The firefighters brought my body up in a basket. When they swung the basket over flat ground they searched for ID. I didn't carry a purse. The trunk on my Vespa had all the girly things needed. My cell phone pouch, that I carried on a strap around my neck, held my driver's license, a bank card, my college ID, and three lonely dollar bills, the leftovers from my last weekend of fun.

"Yabraksha Lilly Leah Mae Tomlinson," a firefighter read from my license.

"I have an awkward relationship with that name," I told Chester. "Its proof positive that parents don't have to be drunk, stoned, or stupid to give a child a difficult name. My college professor parents named me after both their grand-mothers. I always explained it to my friends, 'I was supposed to be twins.'"

"Roxy Tomlinson," the firefighter read my student ID.

"Roxy is easy," I said, and looked to Chester for agreement. He was gone. I started to be miffed that he'd just ghost away without a word. Then I realized he was a ghost. It was okay.

Just then, the sun peeked out from between the mountain and the clouds. In the soggy light of a rain drenched dawn I saw the wrecker truck headed south and the fire truck headed for Fort Bragg.

Before the half-formed thought, 'I want to go home' fully registered in my brain, I was standing in my parent's driveway when the police car pulled in. I saw the officers in the front and a priest in the back as I sliced through the car. They stopped with me surrounded by the trunk. I looked down to see I had a spare tire. Knowing I was far too young for that stage of life, I joined the priest and officers on the porch.

"Roxy?" my mom said as she opened the door. She looked beyond the people at the door. "Oh, sorry, officers, I've always known when Roxy was at the door."

Dad came to the door at the word 'officers'.

"Sorry ma'am," one officer said. Mom invited them in. I watched from the porch swing and listened. The officers gave the details of the accident and the priest offered condolences. The rest of the conversation followed the typical patter of sorrow and support. The light around them tinged a little pink then to a soft red. The redness flowed with them out the door. With no one around to ask about the light, I just watched mom and dad standing in the doorway.

Mom and Dad stood for quite a while holding hands in the silence after they left. Finally, my mother said, "I said 'Roxy?' when I opened the door. I've always felt her presence."

The silence took over until my dad said, "I feel her presence just as if she was perched there on the arm of the porch swing where she always sat."

He pointed right at me and all I could say was, "I'm right here, Dad." Mom looked at me like she heard me and I said, "I'm right here and I'm okay."

An angel materialized between us. I could see him, but didn't think they could. The angel looked just like the pictures in the table top Bible my grandmother had: Big white wings folded neatly behind strong shoulders, long luxurious blond hair, and eyes so blue you could spend half of eternity staring into them. He placed his hands around theirs and the heavenly glow that surrounded him enveloped them.

"Roxy's okay," Dad said. "I can't balance my overwhelming heartbreak at her loss and the peace I feel right now."

My parents went into the house and sat in the middle of the sofa next to each other. That was weird. Dad always sat in the recliner and Mom sat on the end of the sofa near the table lamp. Then the situation got weirder as the angel sat between them like he was holding them on his lap. He wrapped his arms around them and just sat there.

I could only take so much of that. I thought about charging through the door, stomping my foot and demanding, "Are you here to take me to heaven or what?" And there I was with my hands on my hips, stomping my foot like a ten-year-old's temper tantrum and getting ready to ask the question.

The angel looked at me as if he just realized I was there. "Only if you are ready," he said. "Your presence brought peace to your parents before I could get here. I plan to be with them through your funeral next week and for as long as needed after the funeral."

"My funeral?" It was one of those lame half questions, as if I didn't get what was going on. The angel chuckled. (I didn't know they could do that.) He shook his head sadly but smiled. Talk about mixed signals.

"It's not recommended for you to be there?" He answered the question I was only thinking about asking. "No, not the sadness of your friends, but the phoniness. You can see right through them. Have you noticed the aura around the living? It turns from the usual blue green color to pale red when they lie. Deep red when they're really putting on a show."

My mind went in a couple of directions at once. I wondered how many more unasked questions he was going to answer and pondered the red glow that followed the police out the door. I guess they have a job to do. Can't fault them for saying the right words even when they don't mean them.

"Some funerals leave swirls of crimson and scarlet that lingers for days. Yours might saturate for weeks."

"Are my friends that mean and phony?"

The angle laughed. "Fiction and fantasy tend to overwhelm truth and reality at a funeral. Even truth, from an insincere heart, registers red. My recommendation is always stay away."

"You'll be there?" I asked for confirmation. "With them at the funeral."

"And for as many days after as needed," he answered. "At some time, for some sooner, for some later, the peace gets inside, and I'm done."

I tried to formulate a question as I pondered, 'as many days needed.'

"In my realm," he said, "a day could be a thousand years."

There he was again, answering the question before I asked. I started to wonder how he did that but decided I wasn't going to think in questions.

He smiled knowingly. "Go travel. The world awaits. When you're ready, and you'll know when you're ready, call on me and I will take you to the next step."

"When you're ready, you will know my name."

And that was that. I was back on the porch swing listening to its rhythmic squeak and groan.

Okay, no funeral, at least not my own, so travel. I considered the invitations from the reception line. Rejected swamps and moors, and decided on The Mall of America. I pictured myself on the carrousel and I was there. I put my foot in the stirrup and grabbed the pole. As I mounted up, I could feel the coolness of the pole and the pressure of the metal bar of the stirrup.

I tried to understand why I could ghost through a police car and hang on to a pole. The ghost who invited me showed up on my left. She said, "If you want to ghost, you go through, if you want to hang on, you hang on."

I tried to form the words to ask, "Does everyone answer before the question is spoken?" She said, "Yes!" before I could get the words out.

I tried to not think in questions, but too many swirled in my head.

"My name's Amanda. Ride 'til you're bored. I'll introduce you to some others later. Don't touch the live ones. Some of them will see you."

I was thinking about what happened when the mall closed at night, but Amanda didn't give me an answer.

When I said, "What do you do when the mall closes at night?" Amanda closed her eyes and hung her head.

She started to ghost away but I grabbed her hand. She looked up in panic and tried to pull away. Without effort, I held on and pondered how she was not able to break my hold.

"I can't tell you to hide," Amanda said. "Or tell you they like to take the new ones by surprise."

They? I asked myself. Who were they? Then my mind went to Amanda's invitation 'Food, fun, and frolic 24/7.'

"Who has the fun after hours?" I demanded. I tightened my grip on Amanda's wrist. She slapped my hand but I didn't let go. She reached up with her other hand and brought down a meat cleaver. She chopped down at my wrist. I let go, but too late. She faded into the floor, meat cleaver and all. I looked for the bloody stump of my wrist and found my bangles intact. My fingers played scales on an imaginary piano. I hammered out the base notes for Music Box Dancer just to convince myself I was controlling those fingers.

"Humph," I said. "That's one advantage to being a ghost!"

I followed Amanda and found her puddled on the concrete floor. I was gonna wait to confront her until she finished pulling herself back into mall girl form, but five dark figures gathered around her. I held back, lurking between the air-ducts and fire sprinkler pipes near the ceiling. The dark forms coalesced into normal looking mall-rats.

A tall, white boy with a waxed-black mohawk grabbed Amanda's arm and dragged her to her feet. Mohawk wore studded leather wrist bands and a studded black dog-collar. A willowy Asian girl with long straight hair grabbed her other arm. Asia sported crossed Katanas on her back and a long-sleeved, pearl silk gown that flowed to her ankles.

Asia caught Amanda's chin in her hand and leaned close to her face, "I hope, for your sake, you didn't tip this one off." An older boy with a scraggly goatee, pimples, and greasy-brown hair, said, "You know what happened last time!"

Silently, Amanda shook her head in denial.

"She's lying," said the fourth mall-rat.

"Yeah, we always know when she's lying," agreed the last one.

Those two were twins, a boy and a girl. They had light brown skin, curly dark hair, and wore shiny black leather clothing.

Goatee turned on them. I could see him reflected in all four lenses of the mirrored aviator glasses the Twins wore. Goatee demanded, "Do you two every disagree?" He looked at the boy, "Your sister would lie and you'd swear to it." It wasn't a question.

Amanda had lied. She had tipped me off, but I didn't know how the Twins knew.

Everything indicated evil, sorta. You might not cross to the other side of the mall if you saw one of them walking toward you, but you'd duck into 'Maternity Momma's' if you saw two of them coming at you in lock-step. I knew what I saw was sinister.

I studied the Twins. They were too perfect. She wore a miniskirt over leggings with calf-high boots. Her boots showed just the hint of high-heels. He wore his pants bloused over his boots tops. The boots matched hers without that hint of feminine styling. I didn't have time to add up what wasn't adding up, Amanda's cry dragged my attention back to her.

Asia raised Amanda off the floor just by the grip on Amanda's chin. Mohawk let go. Asia slammed Amanda into the wall. "Where did you leave her?" Asia whispered.

"She's on the Carousel," Amanda said. "She won't have any idea until you start the chase. I'll be there to lead her into the trap. I will. I promise I will!"

"You'd better be," Asia said and dropped her to the floor.

The rift between Goatee and the Twins, the Twins perfect match, like costumes in a play, and the almost scripted dialogue, made me think the whole scene was staged. I couldn't tell, evil, or play-acting evil.

Mohawk lifted his foot to stomp Amanda's head and I had seen enough. I did a slide-tackle, soccer style, before Mohawk's foot reached Amanda and dropped him to the concrete floor. I grabbed Amanda and dragged her through the floor and into a parking level below. We didn't stop there. I pushed her into an elevator shaft and then flew up to floors above.

We tumbled out of the elevator shaft through a barrier of caution tape and wooden slats onto a floor where paint-cans and carpet-squares gave evidence of a remodel in progress. The south and west facing windows flamed orange with sunset. I plopped Amanda into an executive chair and got lost in the sunset.

What now and where can we go, chased through my mind. Then, Amanda invited me here, she set me up, she warned me, they threatened her, how do we fight these ghosts, and is this a 'we' fight--whose side is Amanda on?

In the reflection of the plate-glass, the five ghosts formed up in a semicircle facing Amanda. She whimpered, drew her knees up, and wrapped her arms around them.

Asia unsheathed her katanas with grace and style. The Twins peeled razor stars off their jackets. Goatee and Mohawk just stood there as if they would not be needed in this fight.

I am a ghost. I can fade through the floor or jet through the ceiling. I don't have to fight. That was too much thinking. I jumped in front of Amanda and struck one of those karate poses. I never learned its name. Not my fault, really. I got kicked out of the dojo and told never to return. Not my fault, really. I broke four of the instructor's ribs. Well, not an instructor, a sparing partner, Sensei's daughter. She was slapping me around. That wasn't too bad, but she was enjoying it too much. She looked up to see if everyone was watching and left her right side exposed. One hit, really, just one, a left-handed chop, mid-ribcage.

Next day, I was shown the door. Reason, I didn't know how to pull a punch. I ran into Sensei's daughter on my way out and called her a liar about the broken ribs. She said something about spending the night in Emergency. I called her a liar again. She pulled up her blouse. She was taped from armpit to waist line.

Strange what goes through your mind when facing certain death. I hadn't caught up to the idea that I was already dead. There I was in the menacing pose, left hand up, right down, fists open, when the bangles on my left wrists cascaded to my elbow. As if the bangles didn't drive home the idea that a ten-year-old was a little over-matched, Mini squeaked, bowed her head, and put her hands over her eyes.

A moment frozen in time, me standing, waiting for a fight to start that I was sure to lose, when a gallery clap sounded behind me. I tried not to turn, but hazarded a glance.

Quickly, eyes front, stance firm, ready, determined, my brain registered what my eyes had seen. I dropped my hands and turned flat-footed with my back to the attack and stared at Amanda. There she stood, smiling, looking happy and friendly like she did at the roadside reception, giving me a polite little applause as if I had just sunk a 40 foot putt, a nice putt, but not the tournament winner.

"Welcome to the Mall of America," Amanda said.

Then the attackers were upon me. Patting my back and saying, "Yeah, Welcome...Amanda said you were cool...we had to know...what you were made of...You're brave...maybe a little stupid...you should've run...glad you didn't," and other words of friendship and acceptance.

I just stood there, the fear and fight in me draining away to confusion. I didn't think ghosts could cry, but I was wiping tears from my eyes when Mohawk said, "Back off now. Let's give her some room."

Amanda hugged me. I never was big on hugs, but that felt right. She said, "I knew you would fit in."

Fit with this pack of mall rats, I didn't think so. Then I looked up at Mohawk. Different. Hard to say why. Maybe, just the smile. Goatee too. Smiling, relaxed. The Twins had pushed their sunglasses up on their heads and were smiling too.

Asia wasn't smiling. She had sheathed her katanas, but held back from the rest.

"Don't worry about her," Mohawk said. "She rarely smiles and if she does, you'd better run. She hasn't sliced your head off, and for her, that's a sign of real friendship."

Time flows funny in the ghost realm. I joined the mall rats and we had good times. We rode rides and played games. My favorite game was "Ghost in the Machine." I'd sit in the cockpit of the flight simulators and either perfect the aim or mess up a landing depending on the attitude of the pilot. I never figured out how I could influence the electronics of the simulator. I just could.

I was in the middle of helping a little boy perfect a landing when I began to loose touch with my surroundings. I lost control of 'touch or pass through' and ended up on my butt in a cold, dark corner of the parking garage. Amanda was there and a little fuzzy around the edges. Her eyes focused on the concrete wall. I caught a glimpse of a rocky seacoast on the wall. An instant later, Amanda was part of the scene.

I got that feeling like when you know you've eaten something bad and your body is not going to hold it down. I closed my eyes and tried to take a couple of deep breath to steady myself. About the time I realized how useless trying to breath was, I was there on the coast with Amanda.

She said, "I could lie and tell you, you get used to the transition, if you want."

"Transition?" was my foggy thought.

"Yeah, transition," Amanda said. "Every time a new ghost appears where we crossed over, we're dragged back as part of the welcoming committee. Sorta the Ghost Realm's version of the Welcome Wagon."

Rachel and the Hungry Ghosts

Judy Prey

RACHEL RAN DOWN THE narrow wooded path. She quickly looked over her shoulder.

They were gaining on her.

Duh, of course they are, she thought. *Ghosts!*

Long emaciated arms grabbed for her. The ghosts screamed with breath that reeked of rotten cabbage. She stumbled, falling to the rough ground. A hand reached down and lifted her out of the dream.

"Oh, Grammy," Rachel said, jumping out of her bed. "You saved me. I thought those things were going to eat me. I've never seen anything like them."

"There, there," Grammy said, floating at the foot of the bed. "You know I would never let anything happen to you.

Wait." Rachel stopped pacing. "How could I smell something in a dream?"

"Wow, you had smell-o-vision! Good, you're more in tune with your powers, Sweetie. Those ghosts were nasty."

Rachel sat on a chair near the bed. She took a deep breath, and then let it out slowly. "I'm twenty-three. I can handle whatever it is you're not telling me. Come on, Grammy. You've taught me so much. I can feel something's bothering you."

The old woman nodded her head. "Okay, you're right. I should have told you this story before. It's been a mystery that has bugged our family for over a century."

"I don't understand, Grammy. What mystery?"

The ghost floated closer to Rachel. "It all started with my great, great grandmother Sarah Rachel Lamb. She wrote the whole story down in her diary, including the part about seeing ghosts. Anyway, in 1852, her husband Samuel left Sarah and their young son here in Brooklyn and went off to California with his friend Jacob. They were going to make their fortunes in the Gold Rush. Unlike many of the other miners, the two did pretty well. They had a camp near a place up in the mountains called Hangtown. One day, Samuel went into town to get supplies and never returned. His friend looked all over for him. But there was no trace of him and they assumed he was dead. Jacob found more gold and hung onto it. He felt bad about his friend's widow being left all alone with her little child. He returned to Brooklyn and told her about Samuel's mysterious disappearance. Then he gave Sarah half the gold that was left. After a while, the two fell in love and got married. They used the gold to start a dry goods business and did quite well."

"What has this to do with me or my dream, Grammy?" Rachel said.

"Let me finish, dear. Each first-born girl, in our family, is given the name Rachel, either as her first or middle name. We feel and see things others don't. I think knowing you come from a long line of strong women helps you have confidence in your talent. Sarah Lamb wrote about her special dreams in that diary. Dreams are our link to the paranormal. Anyway, it's not something they talked about in those days. Against the Jewish religion and all that. The ones who don't believe can be a real pain in the *tuchas*. Don't laugh, child. Would you rather I say butt?"

"No, Grammy," Rachel said smiling. "I don't understand what all this has to do with me. I'm just a research assistant at the museum."

"My friends here in the ghost realm are worried something evil is growing out west, and it's not that good Mendocino weed I hear about. You need to go to California and find out what's going on. Also, I want you to find out what happened to Grandpa Samuel. I have a ghostly feeling that he's mixed up in what's happening out there. "

"I'll call in to the museum for my vacation time and get a flight tomorrow."

"Good, Sweetie. Have your Mom take care of that stuff. Just tell her the order comes from me. Remember, dear, call out for me if you need help."

After a long, bumpy flight across the country and a quick drive up from Sacramento, Rachel pulled up to her leased cottage in Placerville. She dropped her suitcases in the neat, little living room and stumbled into the kitchen for a glass of water. Sitting at the table was a sweet-faced young girl in a blue polka-dotted dress.

"Hi, Rachel," she said, smiling. "I'm Emily, your house ghost. It's so nice to finally be able to talk to a Breather. As soon as you walked in, I had a feeling you were here to help us. There's some bad ghosty stuff happening on this side. All my spirit friends agree that even the ethers smell bad, like rotten vegetables and meat. Yuck! We're really getting spooked about it."

Rolling her eyes at what passed for ghost humor, Rachel sat down at the table. "Emily, are there a lot of ghosts here in Placerville?"

"Oh, sure. You can forget about the one at the Hangman's Tree Bar and the ones on Prospector Drive. Don't tell them I said that, though. They like to play tricks on their live neighbors, but they're not mean. Those guys love it that people are writing about them. If you go to the Diamond Springs Hotel you can even feel the spirit nexus. That energy is good. We think the bad energy is coming from east of town. None of us ghosts know what to do about it. Do you know anybody here? Living that is."

"Not a soul," Rachel said stifling a big yawn.

"Oh, sorry, Rachel. You look dead on your feet. Get some sleep. Tomorrow, go see John Chan. He's the only one I know personally who can see ghosts. He works for our local newspaper, the *Mountain Democrat*. I played with him at school before I got sick. The paper ran a nice story about how sweet and pretty I was. Anyway, John's cute, and smart, and he knows the area. I think he's maybe your age, like forty."

Rachel's eyes snapped open. "Forty? I'm only twenty-three."

"Sorry," Emily giggled. "I've kinda lost track of time. I was eleven then. Anyway, he can see ghosts, even though he doesn't like to admit it. He came to my wake and I know he saw me waving at him. Tell him I said hi."

The next morning, after another restless night, Rachel sat at the kitchen table toweling off her wet hair and trying not to think of Emily. A sense of urgency told her that this was not the time to be with a chatty kid, even if she was a ghost.

Pulling her iPhone out of her jeans pocket, Rachel Googled the newspaper's number and called for an appointment with John Chan. She still had time to do some chores but she just couldn't get going. How was she going to find the confidence to defeat evil? Just dreaming about it wasn't going to cut it.

"How?" she said to her reflection in the shiny phone. "I'm not as strong as Grammy thinks. Good grief! I look like hell. Now is not the day to go out without makeup."

Rachel walked into John Chan's cubicle office on time. She introduced herself and sat in a chair in front of the cluttered desk. "I'm not quite sure how to start," she said, taking a deep breath. "So, I'll be blunt. I just flew in from Brooklyn yesterday. I met Emily when I moved into her family's cottage on Bedford Avenue. John, she's very worried and told me to get your help. And, she said to say hi. She misses playing softball with you."

John turned pale, stood, and looked over the partition at the busy office. "Miss Klein, Rachel, we can't talk here." He jerked his thumb towards the large room. "They won't understand. Let's go outside." He led Rachel out of the office where they sat on a curbside bench. "Yeah, I saw Emily once and some of the other local ghosts, too. I think my father can see them too, but he doesn't talk about it either. The Chinese have quite a collection of ghosts. Believing in ghosts and actually having a chat with one are two different things."

"John, I had a dream last night that I should tell you about," Rachel said, pushing her long auburn hair behind her ear. "An old Chinese gentleman in an embroidered tunic appeared, standing in a pine forest. There was a storm cloud behind him."

"It's called a *changshan*," John interrupted. "The long silk jacket."

"Oh yes, of course. I did some research for an exhibit of Chinese immigrants at the Brooklyn History Museum where I work. Well, he bowed to me, and said, 'Miss Klein, you will need help in dealing with dark spirits. They have so much hate in them; they won't let *me*, the ancestor of the American Chan family, come near their nexus. Seek John, my great, great, grandson. He will know whom else to ask for aid. Also, tell him I'm proud of him.'"

"Wow, my ancestor said that? Cool!" John's face lit up with a big dimpled smile. Rachel thought Emily was right. He was cute.

"I do know someone we can go see," John rushed on. "Terry Wah is an old family friend. He used to teach Comparative Religion at Folsom Lake College. My car is down the street. I'll call him to make sure he's home."

"Oh, geez! Do you see that?" Rachel asked, grabbing John's arm and hauling him to his feet.

She pointed down the street at a thin specter clothed in tattered pants and shirt. His bearded face was splotched with mud. Leaves and twigs jutted out of his straggly hair. He pointed at them, his dirty fingers grabbing at the shortening space between them. Rooster talons clacked on the pavement and short wings jutted out of his back, too thin to give him flight.

"Sarah," it shrieked.

John blanched. The two fled in the opposite direction towards a black Prius parked on the corner and jumped in. John sped up Main Street. Rachel turned in the passenger seat to see if the ghost was gaining on them. It was still following but losing ground.

"John, he's still there. I'm glad you saw that too. It's not just me."

"Unfortunately, I did. It seemed like it was looking straight at you. Why you?" he said, taking another quick turn.

"I have no idea. Most ghosts I know are nice and friendly." She looked again behind them. "The thing's gone. I could sense how angry it was. Is that what your ancestor warned us about?"

They finally arrived at a large, Tudor-style home. A grey-haired man trimming grass around a statue of Buddha stood up.

"Terry, get in the house," John said, jumping out of the car. "Something weird may be following us."

The three dashed into the house. Terry slammed the heavy wooden door behind them, looking out the peephole. "I don't see anything. What's going on?"

"It's gone," Rachel said, looking out the front window. "I'm not sensing its rage. I've never felt anything like that before. Whoa, Mr. Wah, do you mind if we sit down before my knees give out?"

John grabbed Rachel by the arm and eased her into a chair. "You really do look like you've seen a ghost."

As Terry made tea, John told him about the ghostly visitations predicting doom and being chased by a chicken man screaming English. Rachel was very surprised that the older man didn't scoff at any part of their story.

"My Grammy once showed me a picture book of old Jewish folk stories," Rachel added. "My family was from Poland, where they still believe in spirits and demons. I think that rooster thing was called a *Mazzikin*. It's an evil spirit."

"In other words," John said, "it's a foul fowl."

"As Grammy would say, 'Oy vey.'"

John's joke helped ease Rachel's tension. She noticed an altar near a massive bookcase with two statues, one of Buddha sitting on a lotus and another of the goddess *Quan Yin* floating on a cloud. She felt the goodness the gods personified in this lovely home.

Terry retrieved a well-worn book and leafed through its pages. He laid the open book on the coffee table. It was in Chinese, but the illustrations were easy to understand, and scary. One ghost had spikey hair and angry eyes. Sickly vapors wafted from the spikes. Its skin was sallow and shrunken. Shreds of clothing barely covered it. Another ghost was also shriveled but with long stringy hair and fumes rising from its fanged mouth.

Terry tapped the pictures. "Rachel, have you seen spirits like these?"

"Yes." She shivered in the warm room. "In one of my dreams. Why did you pick them?"

"These particular guys are part of a group called Hungry Ghosts in China and other countries that practice Buddhism. They are malevolent spirits who have smelly hair and breath."

"Like rotten vegetables?" Rachel asked.

"Yes. Right after a person dies, there are many rituals that have to be followed precisely to placate the ghosts. There's a yearly festival to honor the spirits of dead ancestors. It starts August fifteenth. For whatever reason, the wraiths you've seen in your dream were denied those special offerings and prayers. They became angry and transformed into these evil ghosts. All they want to do is create havoc and leach off living energy. I'm worried if they don't return to the lower realm, all hell will break out, literally. Today is August thirteenth. We don't have much time to send them back to where they belong."

"What do you think about the spirit that chased us? Oh, wait a minute," Rachel said eyeing the living room window. "He seemed to be reaching for *me*. I have a very distant relative who disappeared here during the Gold Rush. Could it be him? The old Polish stories said that a Jew deprived of the *Kaddish* prayer for the dead could become a *Mazzikin*. Its anger could cause mayhem and madness." Rachel felt a deep-seated worry settle in her gut.

Terry shook his head. "I don't know. Let's hope we find out when we face the Hungry Ghosts. Sounds like the spirit that chased you has the same problem as these Chinese ghosts, anger issues."

"Could it be as simple as a ritual? What do we do, Terry. I wouldn't know where to begin." John said, his voice firm but with a touch of fear.

Terry nodded his head. "Yes, John. Remember, only a fool pretends to be fearless when dealing with evil. I studied at a Buddhist monastery for a while, Rachel. The ghosts there are pretty chill. Yes, I can see ghosts too. These guys are a whole different matter."

Terry stood to return the book to its shelf. "We have to get the offerings to appease the ghosts. Why are they so pissed off, is the first question. How do we get close to their nexus is the next. The only way we can do that is to have a monk sing special chants. The wraiths don't like the sound and will back off. I'm still a practicing Buddhist, and I have the incense and paper offerings that we'll need. The monks at the monastery in Shingle Springs will help, I'm sure. I'll call them. We have no time to lose. I'll print up the *Kaddish* and a Buddhist chant for you both. Now, go home and get some rest. We'll meet here tomorrow morning. Rachel, maybe you can tap into your sense of the spiritual plane. Get a feeling of where to go. Right now, all we know is that the nexus is east of town."

Rachel shook hands with Terry and noticed his hands were a little sweaty.

Smart man, he listens to his own advice, she thought.

That night, Rachel's grandmother visited her again in a dream. She was in a small clearing in a pine forest, leaning on a large white boulder with black streaks. She said, "Sweetie, don't forget to ask Grandpa Samuel where he's been since

1852. And remember, I'm always nearby. The word on the ghost-vine is that the negative energy is getting worse. There are more murders happening up in those mountains than ever before. Be careful, Sweetie. You're going to have to find the nexus on your own. Dig deep into your perceptual consciousness. Sort of like a sensory dousing rod."

Morning arrived far too early for Rachel. When John picked her up at her cottage, she noticed his eyes were as bloodshot as hers.

"Rachel, we're the good guys. We'll win." He reached for her hand and gave it a gentle squeeze. She realized she didn't want him to let go.

"We'd better," Rachel replied, her voice shaking slightly. With more conviction, she added, "It could be the end of Placerville. Maybe even the world, as we know it. That angry energy is already having an effect on regular people here. It'll spread if we can't stop it. What little I've seen of Placerville, I like. I don't want to see it go up in flames."

Terry was waiting for them outside his house. He ushered them inside. Two saffron-robed men sat in the middle of the room, their shaved heads bowed as they carefully placed the statue of Buddha and pieces of green paper into a wooden box. They stood when John and Rachel came into the room. Rachel followed everyone's lead as they bowed in the traditional Buddhist manner. Terry introduced Master Liu and Master Michael. Rachel liked them immediately. She felt their gentle aura settle her nerves. Taking a deep breath, she told them about her Grammy's message.

"Let's try something," Terry said, pulling a local map out of a side table drawer. He placed the opened map on the floor. "I want you to look into your inner being. Feel the lines of energy coursing around you. Where are they pulling you?"

Rachel knelt beside the map, her eyes closed, hands moving slowly over the paper. Her right finger plunged down onto a small dot. "Do you guys know where Tiger Lily is? That's the nexus."

They all piled into Terry's minivan, with the box safely stowed on the back seat.

Master Liu started chanting, "*Amitabba* Buddha."

Master Michael sang a deeper drone, "*Na mo Ah Mi Tuo Fo.*"

Rachel didn't want to interrupt to find out what the chants meant. Michael seemed to be chanting with an Irish accent. John's eyes were closed while his head nodded to the rhythm of the words. She looked at the printout of the *Kaddish* Terri had given her.

"May His great Name grow exalted…" Rachel spoke the prayer softly. She remembered the words that she said every anniversary of the day her grandmother passed away.

After turning onto Pleasant Valley Road, they all saw a growing fog that shadowed the sun. Terry slowed, and then stopped.

Rachel sniffed the air, looking around at the pine trees along the road. "There," she said, pointing at a narrow dirt track ahead. "I can smell them. I can feel them. They are really creepy! Pull in there."

Master Liu began a slow dispersal chant with Master Michael singing a bass counter harmony. They turned into the lane but could only go a few hundred feet. The lane was now a gravely pathway.

"Please listen very carefully," Master Michael warned as he handed out lit sticks of sage incense. "We must follow our plan faithfully. If something goes amiss, try to keep together. If all else fails, wing it."

He smiled at Rachel's look of surprise. "Yes, I'm from Ireland. I'll tell you my long story after we get these nasty beasties on their way."

The monks increased the force of their chanting. To Rachel, the harmonies seemed to swirl around them. Her skin felt tingly like static electricity. The five piled out of the van. Terry and John carried the box between them.

The cold, slimy air was a tangible power pressing against their straining bodies. Step by step, they pushed their way forward along the path. The smoke of the incense wreathed them like a protective blanket.

After what seemed like hours, they finally broke into a small clearing. A roiling black whirlwind rose from a hole at the base of the white rock Rachel recognized from her dream. She felt the evil issuing from the hole like a hammering in her brain and gut. This was the nexus. The trees surrounding the open area were getting harder to distinguish, fading to ashy grey.

Two giant forms separated from the small tornado. Their clothes were tatters whipping about in the wind, their bodies emaciated. Their odor was gag-worthy.

Terry struggled forward. "*Choukou* Gui, you of the vile breath and *Choumao,* of the spikey hair, why do Hungry Ghosts invade the living realm? What wrongs have been done?" Terry spoke in English, but the ghosts seemed to understand him. Behind him the words of the chants sang counterpoint to his questions.

The two forms advanced. The force of their ranting and heavy, reeking fumes pinned the five humans to the ground. The chants and sage only slowed the wraiths.

Rachel knew the plan was definitely not working when the *Mazzikin* flew out of the hole. His scrawny wings flapped furiously to gain height. Screaming now in Yiddish, he flew about the clearing, pelting them all with pebbles. Not for the first time, Rachel wished she knew more than a few words of her culture's language. She did know that *farkakte* meant shitty.

"Time to wing it!" she cried out, crawling away from the two Hungries and fluttering rooster. "Grammy, we need you." Rachel recited, as loud as she could over all the noise, "May His great Name grow exalted…"

The old woman suddenly appeared before the ghosts, floating on a fluffy cloud. Pointing at them, she said, "I'm not the Lady of Mercy *Quan Yin* arriving to disperse unconditional love. I'm a pissed off Jewish grandmother. What's going on and where is my Grandpa Samuel?"

The two Hungry Ghosts halted their screeching, hovering in amazement. The winds ceased. As if on cue, three more specters crawled out of the hole. They stood shakily and wobbled to where the cloud bobbed about. The men were dressed in plain long tunics and loose trousers. Single long braids fell down their backs. They cowered, frightened by the commotion.

The *Mazzikin* flew lower, then plopped to the ground. He looked at Rachel still intoning the *Kaddish*. He hobbled up to the old lady on the cloud.

"Why do you say the prayer for the dead? Are you family?" he asked, cocking his head from side to side.

"If you're Samuel Lamb you are. I'm your distant grand-daughter, Rachel. Please tell us what happened to you before these two *shmendriks* start up again." She winked at the monks. "Keep singing, boys. That just means jerk."

"Yes, Ma'am, Samuel said. "Early in 1852, I was going to Hangtown to buy supplies for Jacob and me. We had a little camp a few miles from here."

The Hungries roared in anger, interrupting Samuel. They had enough chitchat and family reunions. More dark clouds gathered, churning with streaks of blinding light. A bolt shot out, striking a nearby tree. It burst into flames. Rachel screamed.

One Hungry grabbed Terry and the other grabbed Rachel. They rose up over John's head. He tried to grab her feet but missed. The ghosts threw the humans back and forth, playing toss. Rachel hoped she could hold on to her breakfast.

Grammy rammed the one that held Rachel with her cloud. Stinky Breath spit a large green glob at her, knocking the elderly ghost off the cloud into the air. She landed on her feet near the big rock and then sunk into the ground to her knees as if in quicksand. Samuel rushed over to her, grabbing her arm. The three Chinese ghosts tried to pull on her other arm. They all got stuck in the vile green glue-like goo, pulling Grammy back and forth. Stinky laughed at his handy work.

More lightening flashed, splintering another tree. Spikey sniffed the smoky air and added his cackle to Stinky's.

Rachel's head ached with the thunder and being tossed about in the reeking air. Spikey Hair caught her just as she threw up all over the emaciated hand. The Hungry smiled at her, licking her mouth and chin. She retched again, but there was nothing left in her stomach. She noticed that Terry hung limp in Stinky Breath's hand.

Out of the corner of her eye, Rachel saw John and Master Liu setting up a small shrine with the statue of Buddha and a burner with paper offerings. John's hands shook as he struck a match and just managed to light the fire. He threw *joss* paper into the flames. He looked up to see Master Michael run to a green gelatinous mass of assorted arms and heads while reciting the sacred names of Buddha. The monk waved a bundle of smoking sage around the glued ghosts. The holy words freed the five from their gooey prison.

A deer suddenly raced into the clearing, stopping before it collided with Stinky. The animal shook its head, sneezed, and sped off down the lane. Rachel could see that Terry was finally awake and wiggling about in the ghost's hand.

The three Chinese ghosts strode forward. The men now stood erect, wearing colorful embroidered *changshans*. They bowed to John and the monks and turned as one to the Hungry Ghosts. They said, "Be gone, evil ones. Your hatred makes you stupid. These good people have set us free. We are no longer trapped with your stink. Let those two down."

The Hungries laughed. Spikey lifted Rachel up to his mouth about to bite her head off. She kicked and wiggled, almost breaking loose. Spikey paused to look down. Master Liu and Master Michael both embraced the emaciated legs of the two floating Hungries.

"*Choumao*, you shall release these good people. Thru me, the Lord Buddha commands you. You and *Chaukou* Gui are banished," Master Liu shouted.

Stinky Breath dropped Terry so it could cover its droopy ears with both hands. Still in a daze, Terry crawled to the altar. He placed the last of the offerings on the burner.

The two evil ones screeched, writhing under the touch of the gentle monks. Spikey Hair twitched violently, releasing Rachel. She fell into John's waiting arms and hugged back tightly. After setting her gently on her feet, they turned to watch the Hungries fade and then implode out of existence. Their screams of rage were no longer a tangible pressure.

The air now had a sweet taste. A light rain began to fall, extinguishing the burning trees. Rachel knew in her gut the power of Good had won out over Evil.

The three Chinese ghosts bowed to the monks. "Thank you for rescuing us and honoring our spirits. Now we can ascend to heaven and be united with our ancestors." With that, they rose up into the brightening sky and disappeared.

Terry and the two monks finished packing the box and followed Rachel and John to the big rock where the last two ancestors were sitting.

"All right, Grandpa Samuel. What happened to you?" Rachel asked, pointing to her now normal looking, gold-miner ancestor.

"Well, as I was saying before all hell broke loose, I was on my way to get supplies when I got ambushed by some nasty claim jumpers. They wanted my gold. They shot me and threw my body in that hole. A short while later, the Chinese fellas joined me," Sam said, pointing to his former home. "They got waylaid by the same guys. So, with no one knowing what happened to us or where we were, our spirits were forgotten. We had no one to say the right prayers to honor our passing. We were stuck, trapped in our own little hell, going no place.

"Eventually two of the men got really mad, they changed into those 'things'. We contained them for a long time, but they got too strong for us. Hatred is a powerful weapon. Their hatred infected me. I felt guilty about leaving my family. That opened up my soul to a whole lot of anger the Hungries were spewing out. They went out into the real word hunting for more negative energy to feed on. I guess that's why they're called Hungry Ghosts. They always need more. I went out with them sometimes. I guess I sensed your presence and was drawn to you, Miss. You reminded me of my Sarah and the shame I felt for leaving her. My granddaughter was telling me how well Sarah did. So, thank you all for freeing me. We're going back to Brooklyn to see my old haunts."

Grammy noticed that Rachel and John were still holding hands. "*Mozel tov,* you two," she said, giving them a wink before disappearing with Sam.

The rain felt good on Rachel's upturned face. John took her other hand. "What are you going to do now, Miss Rachel Klein?"

"Well, I think I might stick around and learn more about local history. Maybe you can…"

"Michael, me love. I've finally found ye," interrupted a voluptuous, redheaded ghost floating on a gossamer pink cloud. "You didn't have to leave Kilkenny just because I was dead."

"*Oy*," Master Michael said, turning white as a ghost.

NANI

Caroline Williams

NANI HISSED, ARCHING HER back. Ears flattened to her skull, her tail, bristling with fear as the tremor shook the ground. She faced the approaching lava. A couple of miles away, a lava fountain lit up the pre- dawn Hawaiian sky. The glowing-red sky silhouetted palm trees and the tall slender albizia with their fern-like leafy canopies. The high-pitched night song of the coqui tree frogs was replaced with the roar from the eruption.

Two days ago her family fled the house leaving her behind. It wasn't their fault. Sensing danger, Nani hid in her safe place under the veranda-like lanai that surrounded the house. It was where her family, in happier times, gathered in the evenings enjoying the cool breeze coursing through the open enclosure. The youngest member of the family, Emily, tried to coax her from her hiding place on that fateful day. Nani was too afraid to move. She felt safe in the semi-darkness under the floor planks.

Now she was alone, hungry and still very frightened. Her family had not returned. She missed them terribly. The hiding place no longer offered sanctuary; heated air became stifling and difficult to breathe near the ground. There was no choice. She moved to the lanai where the air was breathable and somewhat cooler. On the lanai, by the back door, stood a small loveseat that would do as a safe place. The sofa was high enough for Nani to wriggle under and gave her a view of the yard.

Feeling somewhat sheltered, Nani peeked out from under the skirt surrounding the loveseat. She watched the yellow-brown glow of spewing lava in the distance. She heard the snapping-crackle of burning trees as the oncoming molten mass devoured them. Nani hissed, emitting a low growl. Rising panic gripped her again when a loud boom burst from the fracture and orange magma rose higher in the air.

The odor of burning wood and plants augmented the rotten egg smell released by the eruption tickled her nose and caused her eyes to water. Nani sneezed and shook her head. She could feel the heat radiating from the flow, now just several yards away from the house.

It was much hotter now and she couldn't feel the cooling breeze that was present earlier that night. Nani felt the urge to flee but her terror told her otherwise. She knew lava surrounded the house and death was near. There was no escape.

She heard the tephra-small volcanic rock and ash-falling on the roof of the lanai. She flinched at the clattering sound. Tephra and strands of Pele's Hair was another reason she retreated to the lanai. The small stones and strands lodged in her paws cutting her pads. They were everywhere on the ground. The roof protected the lanai and her from the falling tephra and strands of Pele's Hair.

The sound of footsteps on the tephra-laden ground startled Nani. She quickly came out of her hiding place, moved to crouch beside the loveseat and began a low trill. Quivering, ready to face any oncoming threat, she waited. A woman came into view walking very close to the flow. She stopped and turned towards the lanai. Standing straight with her walking stick in one hand, she looked directly at Nani.

"Don't be afraid. It is only I, Tutu," she quietly turned away from the advancing magma and headed towards the lanai.

There was something different about her. Nani was puzzled by her scent. The fragrance of earth and the distinctive odor of molten rock, with a hint of flowers surrounded Tutu. A sense of peace and calm flowed from her. Nani felt she should know this grandmother. Nani relaxed her defensive stance as Tutu moved toward the steps.

Tutu made her way up to the lanai and sat down on the loveseat placing her walking stick next to her. She folded her hands in her lap. Nani moved closer with a plaintive meow for help. She rubbed against Tutu's leg and sat back on her haunches looking up at her visitor.

Nani studied the newcomer. The glow from the fountain gave off more light so Nani could make out finer details. The woman's brown face was lined with wrinkles of age, revealing her island heritage. She smiled tenderly as she gazed at the blazing black field before her. Her eyes, a deep brown, held two miniature fountains reflecting the magma spewing from the fissure. Tutu wore a floor-length white dress. A lei of rust-colored flowers hung from her neck. Then Nani noticed Tutu's gray hair turning dark orange with wisps of fire forming a wreath on her head. There was no odor of singed hair.

Nani leaped onto the loveseat, came up to Tutu and began rubbing her head on her arm. Tutu laughed softly and stroked Nani between her ears. The smooth caress of Tutu's hand felt good and it seemed cooler and less stifling now. She sat tall on her haunches enjoying the petting.

Tutu watched the smooth pahoehoe oozing towards them, hissing and popping. Its edges kissed the grass and brush, setting them afire as it progressed. At the closeness of the noise, Nani trembled and a low growl escaped her lips.

"Don't be afraid, Nani. "

Nani was stunned. "*Madam Pele?* "

"Yes, Nani, I am Tutu Pele," she replied. "I came to see how this *section was progressing when I felt your terror."

For a moment, Nani was dazed. The volcano goddess was here sitting next to her. Petting her. Then grief overcame her at the thought of losing her only home and family "*Why, Madame Pele? Why are you doing this? I was happy here. This is my home. I miss my family.*"

Nani yowled with grief.

"I am sorry about having to destroy your home but I need to make some changes to this part of the island. It needs more work." There was sadness in Pele's voice as she continued. "I do regret destroying Kapoho in the process. It was one of my favorite places. That part of my island needed more land. When I'm finished, Kapoho will be a much better place. A place my children will enjoy for a very long time."

Nani sighed. "*I wish I could see it. There is no escape from here. I know I will die soon. The lava is very close now.*"

Madame Pele chuckled. "It is all right, Nani Pōpoki. Your name, Beautiful Cat, suits you. I think you will like your new home with me. You will be happy there."

"*I will?*" Nani said her grief ebbing. "*I like that very much.*"

Pele returned her gaze to the glowing mass of pahoehoe. Nani stood and climbed onto Pele's lap.

Settling herself, Nani no longer noticed the pahoehoe creeping towards them or the flames licking at the wooden steps as its edge started to devour the first step. Instead she closed her eyes and began to purr, dreaming of her new family and home.

THE STRAY

Lee Garrett

T ILLY WORE A TIARA of dragon's breath in her tangled hair, clutching more of the wildflowers that also bulged the pockets of her dress. She strolled downhill in the heat of day, watching twisted banners of smoke rise from her home. Cinders flew in the wind as fire danced up the walls and onto the roof, consuming all that it touched. Watching the blaze, her eyes were wide. She imagined smudgy dragons and flame-shaped goblins dancing in the smoke. Her family was inside. She thought that important—for some reason—but trying to concentrate, her thoughts fractured and melted away as they usually did. Thinking wasn't her *gift in life*, her Papa sometimes said while hugging her. It was why they kept her on the farm, where the mean people couldn't take advantage.

She walked up to the house as it collapsed in on itself, too damaged to support its weight any longer. The flames surged up through the debris, then settled down again to finish feasting.

Tilly sat in the dust, mesmerized by the sight as evening stole the light of day. Finally, hungry, she rocked to her feet. The haze of her mind cleared enough for her to realize that her mother and father were not going to care for her any longer.

Turning her back to the embers, she left the only home she'd ever known. She took the road toward town. She'd never been there before. Momma had said it was dangerous; the priests of Yop'r were there. Poppa called them gort-faced thieves. She had laughed. The words made Momma angry. She'd cautioned Poppa to keep a still tongue in his head so they'd not be cursed. Folks often died under Yop'r exorcism rites and not very well.

Tilly's hunger argued louder than the warnings already fading from memory. She wondered how far town was. Her legs tired, as she marched resolutely on. The first stars of eventide jeweled the sky. Isa, the smallest of twelve moons, cleared the hills. Bright for its size, it slathered the horizon with a silver wash of light. Most of the night would pass before the great moon Jahori crept into view, pursuing her wayward children.

Finally, Tilly came to a place where the forest opened beside the dirt road. There were rough-hewn stones that had once formed a low circular wall. Someone had violently broken it apart. In the center stood a carved image, a man transformed to mystery by the petrified billows of his cloak. The unknown stone-cutter had caught a sense of distance in the figure's chalk-white face, as if the one represented were other than human.

She approached the cloaked figure, reaching out to test its reality. Cold marble met her hand. She snatched back her hand, unsure why. After a few moments, picked up the smaller stones, returning them to the broken wall. Tilly worked steadily until there were no more small stones, just the big ones she couldn't lift. The uneven wall teetered slightly but she was happy with the work.

Kneeling from exhaustion, her sore hands fell into her lap. One hand was cushioned by a pocket. She reached inside, remembering the wild flowers she'd stuffed there earlier. Drawing the flowers out, she smelled their rich floral scent and placed them at the feet of the statue. Wearily, she climbed to her feet; there was no food here, and nothing soft to sleep upon. It was time to go.

She placed her palm against the carved man a final time, wishing him well.

The marble seemed less cold than before. The statue's face appeared less foreboding and remote.

She smiled and returned to the road. Her eyelids grew heavy. Her mind drifted, as her feet kept her on the road of their own accord. Tilly yawned fiercely, covered her mouth a little too late, and stopped without quite knowing why. Her head turned. She saw the statue from the shrine she'd left behind. The stone man sat on a rock, staring at her.

She stared back.

The wind whipped his cloak. She saw the play of muscles beneath his robes as he rose to his feet. This was flesh, not stone—a living man with eyes as distant as the stars.

Her head lifted as he neared. Her eyes locked onto his face. Her heart quickened. Her thoughts remained lost in the arms of emptiness.

He stopped, looming over her. "You provided a service to me but asked for nothing."

"I'm not supposed to talk to strangers," Tilly said.

"That is wise, child, and there are none stranger than I." He bowed. "I am Avryn, the Unknown God."

She curtsied. "My name's Tilly."

"Honored. Now that we're friends, do you want to tell me why you're alone on this road?"

The loss of her family, her home, her life, eluded her, but an echo of pain lingered in her heart. Tears streaked her face. For some reason, she wanted to howl, to keen, and shriek, but her throat closed with sobs.

Avryn stared. His eyes focused on a spot within her head as if he read her thoughts like script on parchment. His brow furrowed, and he took another step. His cape swept around her as he knelt and gathered her in his arms. Her wet face pressed against his chest. Tilly felt him awkwardly stroking her hair as though it were not a thing he did often.

At last, a hug.

"It's all right," he said. "I understand. You don't have to offer words you do not have."

Tilly nodded, then pulled free, forgetting the tears on her face as emptiness returned with greater force. "I'm hungry."

Avryn reached into the shadows of his cape and thrust forth a huge, red globe with golden highlights.

"What's that?" Tilly asked.

"Fuji apple. I get them in the next dimension over. Try it. It's good."

Tilly took the fruit and bit into it. She chewed energetically and swallowed. A sweet and wondrous flavor summoned a smile to her face. She tore into the apple with greedy abandon, vaguely aware of Avryn's fascinated scrutiny. She was finally left with an unappealing core dotted with seeds. Holding it delicately by the stem, she handed it back; from out of the past, she heard her mother's voice telling her: *It's rude not to share.*

Avryn took the core, stared at it, and vented a brief bark of a laugh. In his hand, the core dissolved into red, silver, and green starbursts.

Tilly stood mesmerized by the dancing lights, her mouth hanging open. "Pretty." Her expression saddened as the show ended.

"You'll not reach the town at this rate until morning, and I don't think you can keep your feet that long."

Tilly yawned hugely in confirmation.

"Come with me," Avryn said. "I know a place near here where you will be given shelter. To make sure of it..." He reached again into the shadows of his cape. His hand returned with a gold chain. It was adorned with a red-gold disk stamped with an obscure rune.

Tilly's face brightened again. "Pretty."

"Take it. Even in this Yop'r-blighted land, a few stout souls still honor and fear me. They shall see my sign and know my hand is on you."

Tilly snatched the necklace from his hands and held it closely before her eyes. "Thanks," she muttered, letting her empty hand be taken. Led by Avryn, she ambled along, clutching her prize.

A cold chill passed through her as the road sped underfoot. Every step covered an impossible distance. It seemed they went very far, very fast. The chill faded and they were at a fork in the road. The left branch was wide and rutted with wagon tracks. The right path was narrow, leading in a gentle curve around a hill. Avryn pointed down the right path. "That way leads to a farm. It's not far. Put the necklace on. As long as you keep it near you, I will hear your voice. Call on me in your need, and *terror* shall come to defend you."

Tilly lunged forward, wrapping her arms around her new friend's waist.

He patted her head. "It's all right, Kitten. I won't be far."

She looked into his light-filled eyes as his body turned clear as glass, losing substance. Tilly's hands slid through him as through a dream. His words fell from a whirlwind that dissolved around her, "Run along."

Tilly took the path pressed on her. It brought her to a two-story farmhouse made of logs mired together. Several barns squatted off to the side. Between two of them sat a pen of gort. The tubby animals glowered at her with mean red eyes as she passed. They grunted comments to each other, clawing up the ground. In the yard around her, wingless birds wobbled from her path on stubby legs, hissing their irritation. The front door to the farmhouse opened. A huge, burly man appeared with lantern in one hand and an ax in the other. Through the haze of light, Tilly saw his face distorted by a grim scowl. "Who's there?" he called.

"I am," Tilly said.

The man's brow furrowed. His scowl deepened as he advanced a few steps. His eyes locked onto Tilly, widening with disbelief.

"Yop'r's bloated rump, Myra! It's some fey sprite, or I miss my guess."

A large-boned matron appeared behind him, wiping callused hands on an apron. She brushed a silver lock of hair from her eyes, peering past her husband. "'Tis no night-born spirit, Yoris. It's a child! Bring her in."

"Not so fast." He stared off into the darkness behind Tilly. "There are wily bandits in these hills. She could be bait in some trap."

"Caution in these times is proper, husband, but if you look closer at the girl you will see she bares a sign all too rare these days."

Tilly watched Yoris' eyes lower to the medallion she wore. A strange expression stole over the man's face, as it drained of blood. He lowered his ax and bowed with urgently recalled courtesy. "We are honored to receive you in the name of your patron." He gestured toward the main door of the house. "Come and be welcome to all that is mine."

Weary, the dozen steps to the threshold looked like the miles she'd already crossed. She felt strange, unaccountable tears on her checks as the farmer's eyes came back to her face.

"I'm hungry," she said.

Yoris straightened and lurched forward, staring deeply, as if discerning the scars upon her soul. His massive arms gathered her up gently.

She sensed a sudden burst of love mixed with pity within his heart. People were usually unfathomable mysteries to her. *How odd.*

She was carried into the house and deposited at a table where six boys of staggered ages sat at dinner, battling ravenously for food though there was plenty on the table.

"Everything all right, Father?" the oldest boy asked, a heavy golden lock of hair falling into his face.

Tilly wanted the boldness to brush it back in place. She trembled deep within, where something newborn wanted to break free. Were the boy a flower, she'd pick him and keep him in her pocket forever.

Yoris answered, "'Parently so, Judd. This little thing was all that stirred the gort. Be nice to her—I mean it—all of you."

"Poor thing," Myra returned to the table with a clean plate. "She looks like she's nearly done in." She filled a plate, batting away the boy's questing hands to get to the food, and set the plate before Tilly. She gnawed a strip of gort meat, letting its juice drip down her chin. The pleasure of the taste drew a happy sigh, as her gaze wandered.

"She's a rude one," the smallest boy said. "Not even a *thank you.*"

"Hush, Kori," Yoris said. "The girl's a bit touched in the... er...ah...well, just don't trouble her about such things."

The table grew still as the gort outside kicked up a new ruckus.

"What now?" Yoris rolled his eyes toward the rafters. "Am I destined never to finish this meal?"

He left the table. A moment later, Tilly heard the creak of the door. It slammed. There was a flurry of activity as it was barred as well.

"What is it?" Myra called through the wood.

"The accursed priests of Yop'r. They've come for tribute."

"Why? They know we won't pay them," Myra said. "We never have."

Absently, one of Tilly's hands caressed her medallion. Her thumb traced the pattern on its face, and her thoughts cleared a little, crystallizing. "They've come for blood." Quickly, she snatched a biscuit from someone's plate. "They're the ones who burned down my home."

"I was going to eat that," Kori complained, "and there aren't any more!"

Tilly blinked, plucked a fistful of wildflowers from her dress pocket, and deposited them on his plate, a fair exchange.

Kori's face reddened. He opened his mouth to rage, but was stopped by Judd's hand on his shoulder. The older boy glared and shook his head in warning. "Leave her be. She needs the biscuit worse than you. Here, take mine."

Tilly's gaze slid to Judd.

He smiled at her.

Her face warmed as she stuffed the biscuit in her mouth.

"Judd!" Myra called.

"Yes, Ma'am?"

"It's time again. You know what to do."

"Yes, crawl through the tunnel to the gort pen, open the gate, and encourage them to run amok, while Father distracts the priests."

"Aye, it's worked before, it should now. Get going. They'll be banging on the door soon."

Driven by an alien impulse, Tilly pushed away from the table. She padded in Judd's wake, becoming his shadow as he paused to pull a cabinet away from the wall. A hidden space was revealed. Judd stomped down a flight of stairs, swallowed by darkness. She followed, her hand sliding along a railing.

The blackness clung like a cocoon. She pushed through it, chasing the echo of Judd's footfalls. Cool, fetid air assailed her. She stumbled onto another flight of stairs, bruising herself. Her breath slammed out of her. Her thoughts grew thinner, more distant than usual, as she scrambled up the stairs and out onto a trapdoor that lay in a thick patch of shadow. She sensed someone just before her, crouching next to a feed bin. Judd. She watched his shadow-shape slip through a fence of rough-hewn logs and into a huddled, shuffling mass of gort. The animals accepted him without complaint. He patted them and scratched the hide behind their ears. They gave him cover as he moved to the front gate.

A moment later, the gate swung open. Judd imitated the cry of a wounded baby gort and leaped clear as the herd instantly turned murderous. They thundered out of the pen, saw a cluster of priests bearing torches near the farmhouse door, and veered for them.

Tilly wandered over to the fence and leaned against it, watching as the priests were mauled and trampled. They screamed with high, ragged voices as bones snapped and blood spurted from torn flesh. The carnage was not pretty, but Tilly watched, having nothing better to do until Judd appeared beside her. Her eyes swung to his face and remained there.

He said, "You shouldn't be out here. Pa will be pissed."

Tilly continued to stare silently.

Judd sighed and took her arm. "Come with me. The trouble's over. We can go in now. There's no use trying to pen the gort up again until they calm down."

Tilly allowed him to guide her toward the farmhouse. She stepped over scattered bodies, skirting the main cluster of gort. She and Judd were nearly to the porch when a half-dead priest thrust up in their path. Blood dripped from his shattered nose. He clutched a carved crystal wand, mouthing curses mixed with arcane incantations.

Judd swept Tilly behind him.

She stumbled and fell. Looking up, she saw the wand spew a thick jag of violet-white fire.

Judd cried out as the fire swatted him away in a high arc. He fell heavily and lay still.

A sharp pain pierced her heart. She tasted white-hot fury for the first time in her life.

One hand clutched her medallion, as she turned to the priest. Her other hand went flat to the blood-drenched ground.

The priest pointed the wand her way. Violet-white fire surged at her. It was rolled back by the earth bucking up, shaping itself into a giant hand. The fire only hardened the hand, making it stronger as Tilly climbed to her feet. Staggering forward a step, she made a grasping gesture, and the earthen hand snatched up the priest, enclosing him in a fist. Slowly, the fist sank into the ground, pulling the priest along. Soon, the ground was smooth and unbroken and the priest lay buried, choking on the loam.

The girl walked over to Judd and stood over him. His body sprawled, limp, arms and legs at unnatural angles where bones had snapped. This wasn't right; her momma had always told her to take good care of her toys. Tilly studied Judd. The medallion warmed in her grip. Judd's limbs straightened, mending. His chest expanded with a huge draw of breath. His eyes opened wide.

He sat up. "I dreamed I was kilt!"

She nodded.

"That's crazy," he said.

She nodded again.

"What happened? Where's that priest?" The lock of hair was back in his face.

She brushed it back for him. "I buried him."

"Then...he's dead."

"Nearly."

Judd closed his eyes, shuddering. "Remind me not to make you mad."

"Don't make me mad."

He gave a weak laugh. "Uh, thanks."

"I'm sleepy," she said.

He nodded. "Sure, let's go in."

Tilly smiled as Judd levered himself to his feet. His family closed in. His parents hugged him fiercely. The other children babbled excitedly, swarming.

Myra fingered his scorched shirt. "Judd, are you all right?"

"I think so." He pulled away from everyone, returning to Tilly. A puppet, he moved on unseen strings, leading her toward the house. An idea found its own way into his head. "You can have my bed if you want."

The front door opened before her, untouched by human hands.

Like a dark, faint wind in the distant trees, Tilly heard the laughter of the Unknown God wishing her good night.

Church in the Wildwood

Chris Crowe

HANK PULLED INTO THE parking lot of "The Office," a seedy bar on the 49 south of I-20 near Dixie Gardens. The gravel crunched under the tires of his 4x4 Chevy Silverado. The warm touch of the morning heat gave promise of a sweltering Louisiana July day as he opened the door and stepped down out of the truck. He entered through the plywood slab doors and waited until his eyes adjusted to the dark before starting down the brick steps.

As usual, everyone in the bar turned to see who entered. Talking stopped when they saw Hank.

As his eyes adjusted, Hank noted some oilfield workers sitting in the first cubicle and Willie and Wonka, the Opelousas Twins, sitting in their regular cubicle in the far-right corner. The Office didn't have booths. They had cubicles.

Skinny Williams stood behind the specially built bar designed to accommodate his six-foot-eight, 400-pound frame. Oui-Oui Ouimet, the blond bargirl in a short, Grant Tartan, skirt leaned on a barstool to Hank's left. Her lanky frame and big green eyes made it seem as if she had been lifted out of the pages of anime. She was Cheryl's friend and Hank knew he would have to tell her what was going on.

Hank took the six steps down to the main floor and sat next to Oui-Oui. He had just finished telling her how he had put Cheryl in an out-of-state rehab when the doors opened and Phillip, Hank's brother-in-law, stepped in.

Phillip didn't wait until his eyes adjusted to the dark. He missed the third step and stumbled into Hank's arms.

"I should'a let you run smack into the bar," Hank said as he straightened Phillip up and placed him on the barstool next to him.

"Best you didn't, Harold, 'cuz I might not have warned you that Cheryl's brothers are out to git you."

"How would they know I was here?" Hank said. "This is so far off my regular haunts."

"I figured you'd be talking to Oui-Oui, so I came out here looking for you. I called Joe-Joe and Billy when I seen your truck in the lot. I'll bet Billy called the rest."

"You mean you're carrying water for Cheryl's whore-mongering, dope-dealing, ex-con half-brothers? The same ones you've nothing more than cursed all the years I've known you?"

"Harold, you better watch what you say about them Clark boys. 'Cuz nobody's got your back."

"Phil, I've always been fond of you because you're Cheryl's baby brother, but you call me 'Harold' one more time and I'll take you out back and beat you like a dusty rug. Only my mother calls me 'Harold.'"

"No matter, you just better start telling us what you done with Cheryl."

"Where Cheryl is and what I've done is none of your concern or theirs. And if by 'us' you mean you, and the Clark boys, just remember, 'birds-of-a-feather get shot gunned together.'"

Hank slid off the barstool, straightened his 6'4" frame, and pushed Phillip back down when he tried to stand up.

"You sit back down and get real drunk. You're too stupid sober."

Skinny looked over at the commotion and gave Hank a quizzical look. "Everything okay over there?"

"Yeah, Skinny, here's forty. That should be enough to get him real drunk. I'll cover cab fare if that's not enough." Hank placed two 20's on the bar and anchored them with his empty mug.

Phil studied the money until he caught Skinny's eye. "I'll take another," Phil said, and wrapped his hands around the empty mug.

Outside the bar, Hank blinked while his eyes adjusted. He saw Phil's broken down Corolla parked in the handicapped space near the entrance. Reaching for the hunting knife in his boot, Hank thought, *to slow him down, I should slash all four tires on Phil's car, but with the handicapped plates, it's hard to tell which one is the cripple, Phil or car.* Rejecting the idea, Hank sheathed his knife.

Before Hank reached his truck, Joe-Joe Clark pulled into the parking lot in his rusty El Camino and parked behind Hank's Silverado. He rolled down his window but didn't get out.

"You're gonna tell us where you put Cheryl," Joe-Joe said in a friendly conversational tone.

Hank gave him a crooked grin but didn't answer.

Joe-Joe recognized the grin. He and Hank had run the swamps together as kids and fought side-by-side against half the boys in the Parish. Even the older boys learned, when Hank quit talking and started smiling, it was a good time to practice the better part of valor.

"This isn't a fight you can win, Hank," Joe-Joe reasoned. "This is four against one."

"Five to one if you count Phil," Hank said.

"No one's counting Phil," Joe-Joe said. "He came out on his own."

Hank walked to his truck. He reached behind the seat, pulled out his Glock 19 and stuffed three clips in his pockets. He grabbed his shotgun off the rack and picked up a box of shotgun shells.

Joe-Joe stepped up behind him. "Those won't help."

Hank turned to face him. "Cheryl is in rehab out of state, under another name. You won't find her. If I told you, Brother Billy would make sure she got the pills just like the last time."

"Billy was just trying to help when the doctor cut her off," Joe-Joe said.

"Not without reason. She was Billy's connection to Caddo Heights. When Judge Hamill's wife wanted pills, she reached out to Cheryl. Mrs. Hamill knew Cheryl had a supply even through the doctor had cut her off. Billy had the inside track to the richest drug market in the Parish."

Joe-Joe grimaced and turned away.

The roar of pickup trucks interrupted the moment.

"Run!" Joe-Joe shouted. "That's Billy and he's not alone!"

Hank shot a glance toward the far entrance. Billy cut into the lot at high speed, kicking up dust and rocks in the gravel lot. He fishtailed, gunned the engine, and slid to a stop blocking the exit. Three more pickups screeched into the parking lot blocking all exits.

"Run!" Joe-Joe shouted. He pointed toward the side of the bar. "They won't shoot with me in the line of sight."

Hank backed away with the Glock in one hand and the shotgun in the other. He turned at the dumpster and ran down a deer trail into the piney woods.

Shots pinged off the dumpster. Hank looked to his left and saw Cliff Crowder firing off another round. Hank laughed and sprinted deeper into the piney woods. *Cliff never hit anything he aimed at* was the thought that generated the laughter. Recalling Cliff killing Old Tomlin's prize Holstein by accident motivated the speed.

Shots from other directions whizzed by as Hank ran. He plunged into the piney woods on his right to avoid the swamp at the end of the trail and stumbled through the underbrush until he stopped hearing gunfire.

I can't be lost. I know every deer-trail and footpath on both side of this swamp. He crept on quietly trying to make as little sound as possible while listening for pursuit. His confusion grew when he stumbled into a wide, rutted, road that looked like a covered wagon trail.

Swamp's to the left. Highway has to be to the right. I'll circle back to the bar. If I can't get to my truck, I'll hitch a ride out of here.

Listening for sounds of pursuit, he turned toward the highway. After only a few steps, he heard a sound more troubling than someone crashing through the woods: Billy's Kawasaki Brute Force 750 Quad roaring down the trail. The souped-up quad mounted two high-powered spotlights and a laser-sighted British 303 on the handlebars. In season or out of season, Billy didn't miss.

Hank leaped over a blackberry bramble and sprawled out on the ground. He spooked a doe and two fawns that darted out of the bramble, but a big buck just stood there looking at him like he was more a curiosity than a threat. Billy braked hard to miss the deer and stopped. He cut his engine and pulled out his cell phone.

Hank crawled to where he had line-of-sight on Billy's leg with his Glock, but didn't pull the trigger. *What is he doing with the cell?*

Hank got his answer when his cell started playing *Scotland the Brave.* Hank shifted the Glock to his left hand and reached to the phone clip on his right hip to silence the phone.

Billy fired and silenced the phone before Hank reached the clip. Hank patted his belt checking for a smashed phone and blood. He found neither.

The buck bounded away from the gunfire and crashed through the piney woods.

"I got 'em now!" Billy shouted. He fired up the quad and charged off the path in pursuit of the buck.

Hank followed his target as Billy rode past. He didn't fire. Billy was Cheryl's brother. She wouldn't have minded much if he had capped Billy when he fired at him, but she was not likely to forgive a back-shot and that was all he had now.

Hank waited a few moments until the quad got away then he retrieved his cell. It was insured against all damage. *Wonder how Sprint will try to weasel out of a bullet gouge across the back. Can't charge me for the screen. It's not broke.*

Working to get a shot at Billy coming towards him, Hank followed the swath cut by the quad deeper and deeper into the piney woods. Then, the sound of the quad creeping toward him gave him hope. The quad's path crossed a deer trail. The trail took a sharp right turn a few yards from where Hank stood. Thick brush blocked the view around the turn. Hank sensed the quad was coming down the trail. Then it stopped. The engine shut off.

Hank froze. The first one to make a sound would die. Listening intently, Hank hoped to get a bearing from the quiet clicking of a cooling engine.

At first, bug sound was all he heard. Loud, all-encompassing bug sound. Then Hank started filtering out sounds and focusing on what he wanted to hear. He started concentrating on where he last heard the quad.

He'd never given much thought to his ability to filter out noise and focus on what he wanted to hear until one night at a bar down in Mobil. He'd said, "The fiddle is off, but the lead guitar is hot."

"Like you can tell," Joe-Joe scoffed. "The band's thumping and the ventilation fans are blasting, not to mention a bar full of rowdy cowboys and you can tell a fiddle is out of tune?"

"You can't?" Hank asked.

"I got a brand new Benjamin, says you've had a beer too many," Joe-Joe said.

At the break, Joe-Joe caught the band coming off the stage. Hank watched as Joe-Joe talked and pointed his way. Joe-Joe walked back shaking his head and muttering to himself. He peeled off a c-note and stuffed it in Hank's pocket.

A few weeks later, Joe-Joe and Hank walked into the new mall in Montgomery. "Why they playing that sappy music? Doesn't their DJ have better than a classical string quartet in his stuff?" Joe-Joe griped.

"It's live," Hank said. "Guess Montgomery's going high class."

"I got a Benjamin ..." Joe-Joe started to challenge Hank. "No, double or nothing on the bar bet," Joe-Joe finished.

When Hank didn't take him up on it, Joe-Joe said, "Chicken!"

"You're on," Hank said. "Follow me."

Joe-Joe peeled off the bills, but that was the last bet he lost on Hank's hearing. For months after, Joe-Joe would prompt Hank to make some outrageous comment on the music or the make of a car engine and then bet with him against the locals and visiting yokels.

Hank just smiled when he caught the snap and pop of the cooling engine. He holstered the Glock and unslung the shotgun. Just before pulling the trigger, another sound distracted him. The sound came faintly from just beyond the cooling engine.

Did Billy turn on church music to confuse me? No, the music's live. That can't be, not out here. Hank closed his eyes to concentrate on the music.

Focused on the music, Hank didn't hear the starter engage. The roar of the engine caught him by surprise. Billy raced into sight. Hank jerked the shotgun up, fired, and missed.

Billy gunned the engine to run him down. Hank jumped out of the quad's way and turned to fire.

"Back shot or not, I'll kill you!" Hank shouted and pulled the trigger. At that instant a bullet hit the top of Hank's barrel. The shotgun blast kicked up the dust at the quad's back wheels.

"I got him! I got him, Billy!" Cliff shouted a little before the fact.

Hank didn't wait for Cliff to get it right. He ran zig-zagging through the piney woods. He ran with purpose not panic. He stopped before he was winded and crouched down to listen. The wind brought the sound of frogs and insects playing out the circle of life and the church music.

Hank waited until he was sure no one followed and closed in on the organ music. As he got closer, he heard "Nearer My God to Thee" wafting on the breeze. Laughing, Hank thought, Getting shot could *bring that a lot closer.* He came to a wide, well-traveled path that curved away to the right toward the music.

Hank followed the path. *I thought I knew every inch of these woods, but never came upon this trail.* The curve of the path kept the end just out of sight. He followed the sound and when "Nearer My God to Thee" stopped, he stopped and looked back. The path behind him was gone.

Fear and anger fought to force Hank into a panic. He took a deep breath to control his breathing and gain control of his emotions. *Panic in the woods will never do.*

"Farther Along You'll Understand Why" seemed to come from just a few steps around the curve. Anger won. Anger at Billy for getting his wife strung out on pain meds, anger at the disappearing trail, anger at the music being just out of reach. Hank checked his Glock. Slammed home a fresh magazine and charged around the corner and stopped. *I'm lost. I know I'm lost. I've never seen this clearing much less that old clapboard church at the end of the path.*

He studied the church. The aged brown boards had never been painted, yet had the look of a well-built edifice. Hank approached with caution. The steps didn't creak and the doors didn't squeak as his entered.

An old, white haired man in worn overalls greeted him with a smile, "You won't be needing that piece in here, Brother." His friendly smile put Hank at ease.

Hank followed the man's gaze to the Glock. He realized he had his finger on the trigger. He quickly indexed his finger and slowly let his arm drop.

The old man held out his hand in welcome. Hank holstered the Glock and shook the man's hand. The man guided Hank to an empty back pew and Hank sat down and looked over the congregation, women in bonnets, girls in pigtails, boys and men in faded coveralls and plaid shirts. All had the look of an 1800's country church. The song shifted to, "Amazing Grace how sweet the sound that saved a wretch like me ..."

I might be a wretch, but I'd feel a lot less wretched if I'd hit Billy with both barrels. His thoughts shifted to Cheryl and he knew he couldn't sell that to her.

The tempo shifted with a new upbeat song, "Fear not for I have redeemed thee, I have called thee by name." *God, if there is a God, has never called me by name!* Hank thought. Then, a memory from years ago in Sunday School, challenged that thought.

The memory of being the heathen kid from the wrong side of the tracks finding welcome and acceptance at the big formal church downtown.

The song changed again. And now children's voices sang, "Jesus loves me this I know, For the Bible tells me so." While the children sang, the minister, invited people, troubled in soul and mind, to come forward for prayer.

Hank took a step. *Prayer for Cheryl can't hurt.* At the front he joined a group of people kneeling at a wooden bench. From his Sunday School days, he recalled the bench was called an "altar."

Hank tried to organize his thoughts into prayer. Cheryl, the accident, the surgeries, the pills, Billy, Joe-Joe, and then more pills, addiction, jumbled together and refused to form a coherent pattern.

Hank turned his thoughts from the jumble to God. He closed his eyes and prayed a simple prayer, "God, I don't know what to do, I don't know what I need, but You know what I need, and I'm asking for it."

The murder in his heart melted into peace. He reached to his Glock and placed in on the altar in response to the peace that flooded through him. He didn't understand how God could replace the turmoil of his soul with such overwhelming peace. *The accident, the surgeries, the pills, the addiction are all still there, but it's like God is saying, "I got this, Hank. You can let go."*

Hank opened his eyes to a sensory onslaught that brought confusion to his mind but didn't diminish the peace in his heart.

Hank couldn't tell which sensation came first, the setting sun, the cool breeze, the chorus of insects, or the wet grass soaking through his jeans at the knees.

The church with all the singing people and the hardwood floor was gone. He knelt in Ford's Meadow about twenty yards from the edge of the swamp. Three burnt-out Model A's that gave the meadow its name, maintained their silent vigil near the water's edge.

Hank studied the rusted hulks and recalled the story Grandpa Morris told about how the Moonshiners set the ambush for the G-men. The stolen Model A, the chase, the shootout, the explosion, and nobody died.

Hank stood and laughed at the memory. He walked slowly around the meadow searching for the Church in the Wildwood. *I guess I'll join the ranks of the crazies. The congregation of those who tell of angels, miracles, and The Church in the Wildwood just got another member. The only trace of the church is God's peace still in my heart.*

Hank found the path along the swamp that led back to the bar. He stopped at the edge of the lot and saw that Billy's truck blocked his in. He reached for the Glock and looked back along the path. *Oh, yeah. I left the Glock on the altar. Yet, if I don't face Billy down now, he will keep coming after me.*

Hank entered the bar through the delivery door in the back and entered behind the bar. He waited until his eyes adjusted before he moved any further. Oui-Oui Ouimet saw him and immediately looked to the cubical where Billy and his cronies sat.

Hank pulled Skinny's double-barrel shotgun from under the bar, stepped over to Oui-Oui and whispered, "That tray for them?" She nodded and backed away.

Neither Billy nor his friends noticed when Hank set the tray on the edge of their table. They each grabbed a mug and continued talking.

"Anything else I can get you boys?" Hank smiled his crooked little smile while he waited for their reaction. A hundred or so things happened in the next few seconds.

"Nah, we're good," Billy said without looking up.

Big Mike looked up, gagged on a mouthful of beer, and spewed it all over Billy.

Reacting to the spray, Billy knocked his beer sending a flood into Big Mike's lap.

Cliff, sitting next to Billy, reached for his revolver, smacked the underside of the table, and fired off a round. The bullet grazed the heel of Cal's boot before splintering the oak floor.

Cal and Big Mike leaped up ripping the table top off its pedestal, toppling beer, mugs, and the bar-mix bucket on to Cliff and Billy.

Billy and friends wrestled with the table top. Hank side-stepped as they sent it sliding across the floor. The table top hit the bar with such force that it ricocheted back. Billy flopped out of the way. Cliff never saw it coming. The table smacked Cliff's gun hand fracturing three fingers and discharging another round through Cal's cargo pants pocket.

Cal's fist connected with Cliff's jaw dropping him back into the seat. "Shoot me or don't but leave my new Galaxy out of it. That phone cost a lot of money!"

The bar got really quiet with everyone waiting for what's next. Billy scooted away trying to get away from Hank and bumped into the bar. Hank turned on him. *This has turned out better than I'd planned. I've got him trapped between two barstools.*

"Hold, hold," Billy held up his hand, pleading.

"Okay," Hank said. Shifting the shotgun away he reached down to help Billy up.

Billy snapped his head back trying to get away, slammed his head into the bar, and knocked himself out.

Hank turned to Billy's friends. "You take care of Billy and when he wakes up remind him I didn't kill him."

Setting the shotgun on the bar, Hank reached down to remove the carabiner with Billy's keys from his belt. When he turned toward the door, Big Mike growled, "You're not just gonna walk away."

"Yeah," Cliff moaned as he shifted his gun toward his left hand. The gun clattered on the floor. Cliff moaned again as if by reflex he reached for it with his right hand.

"Best leave it," Hank said. "Third time might not be so charming for Cal."

Cal scooted the gun away with his foot when Cliff looked down trying to locate it.

"I'll lay it out for you, Big Mike," Hank said and pointed to the shotgun on the bar. "I could've served you a double-barrel instead of beer." Hank laughed as he watched them looking at the shotgun. "You guys set out to kill me."

"We never planned on killing," Big Mike said. "Billy just wanted to know where you stashed Cheryl."

Staring Big Mike in the eyes, Hank said, "You know that won't happen."

Big Mike's eyes flitted toward the bar and then back to Hank's stare. Hank followed Big Mike's glance. Billy had reached up and grabbed the shotgun. He fumbled with the hammers and finally pulled both back.

In the seconds when Billy swung the shotgun up to target Hank, Big Mike grabbed Cliff and pulled him to the front. Cal leaped over the divider into the next cubical flopping onto the young couple trying to mind their own business. Cal sprawled across the table scattering bar-mix, drinks, and Cajun fries.

Billy shouted "Boo-yah" and pulled both triggers.

"Boo-yah? Really?" Hank laughed and tossed two twelve-gage shells into Billy's lap. "Works better with these," he said and walked toward the door.

While Billy grabbed for the shells, Big Mike kicked the shotgun out of Billy's hands, and sent the gun skittering across the floor. Billy scrambled after the shotgun. Big Mike grabbed him by the collar and helped him up.

"It's over, Billy," Big Mike said. "With you and Cliff chasing through the woods and shooting up the countryside it's a wonder there's no bodies laying out there and that you are not in the Parrish jail on murder charges. Bigger wonder is that you're not waiting on the coroner and Hank's not in jail. He could'a killed you before you knew it and got the rest of us besides."

"Yeah, Hank, what's that all about," Billy called to Hank before he reached the door. "Why didn't you kill me? You had your chance."

"I've been to the Church in the Wildwood," Hank said without emotion or explanation.

Billy scoffed, "That can't be real. The Church in the Wildwood is just a story told in these parts."

"I'll tell you just how real it is, Billy, you're still breathing," Hank said. "And every breath you take from now on is proof of the peace God gave me as I knelt at the altar in the Church in the Wildwood."

"Peace?" Billy questioned, more to himself than to Hank.

"Yeah, Billy, peace that I don't understand," Hank said. "I can't describe it to myself, so how can I tell you? You remember church camp back before middle school? That evangelist from Biloxi said, 'Only God can give you peace that passes understanding, but you've got to be in circumstances you do not understand to get it.'"

Out in the Cold

Leonard Little

L IZZY AWOKE COLD AND alone. Dew had settled on her face as the night approached its end, waning toward the morning. She pushed herself up into a sitting position, but her body didn't move with her. It remained as it was, prone, the cold air drawing the last remnants of heat from her flesh making her appear even paler than the death that claimed her.

Oh my God! Lacy…She's at Mom's…She'll be devastated.

Lizzy's mom watched her daughter when Lizzy was on the job, unless it was her ex's turn to take her.

Oh crap, now Wayne'll get full custody. My poor baby.

He was the self-centered ass who cheated on Lizzy with every woman that looked his way.

Lizzy closed her eyes and shook her head at the sheer idiocy of her not preparing better for her death. She was an investigator for the Placer County Sheriff's department out of Auburn, California.

Damn. I wonder if that's why my spirit is still here?

Death did not reveal the answers she'd hoped it would. All she had were questions, like What had happened to me? How did I get here? She didn't even know where here was.

The loud roar of a semi-truck using its engine brakes on a long downgrade told her she was close to a highway somewhere in the hills, but where? She hoped she wasn't far from home, but one way or the other she had to find out what or who had done this to her. So, she got to her feet finding it so much easier than it had been before. A lot easier than it had been the last three years when a skiing accident left her with an ache that, until now, had bothered her every time she shifted weight to her injured knee.

Her hand flew to cover her open mouth as she caught sight of the condition in which her body was left. Her blouse had been torn open and her bra pulled down, exposing her to the elements. Her pants and panties were gone, leaving her bottom half bare. She didn't remember any of it. The last thing she recalled was leaving the station when her shift ended. Everything after that was a complete blank.

Lizzy investigated homicides, suicides, accidents, child abductions, and anything else that crossed her desk. The investigators were spread thin over a territory that reached from Roseville to Tahoe City, including part of Lake Tahoe at the Nevada border. She'd seen several bodies, some mangled beyond recognition, but nothing could prepare her for seeing her own homicide. The sole reason Lizzy was an investigator was because her father had been murdered when she was eight. She was the first to discover his body on the front lawn of their home.

After the shock of seeing her own body had worn off, she let the rest of her emotions drop away, so she could study the scene. In life she used to pretend to step out of her body every time she was faced with the horrors of her job. It let her focus on the details of the crime. Emotions were great once you knew who the perp was, because they pushed you to put the bastard away, but they got in the way when it came to figuring out who did what and why. She laughed at the irony of her actually stepping out of her body this time. The trick worked just as it had in life, letting her mind work unhindered by the absurdity that she was now trying to solve her own murder.

The first thing she noted was how her body was displayed. Her legs were spread apart as if she'd been raped right there on the ground, but the earth beneath looked barely disturbed. The telltale signs of toe and heel marks from boots or shoes were missing along with palm prints on either side or her pelvis.

The scene was staged, but why?

She let that question drop for a moment, and continued her examination, knowing she would come back to it later. It wasn't good to fill your mind with possible answers until you had all the facts. Or at least as many as you could find before it was time to put the case together. She knew an investigator who hung his whole case on one lead and missed the real murderer until he killed again.

Lizzy continued to study the scene. She tried to check for signs of rape, but her spirit-hand passed right through her real body as if it weren't there. There was an injury through the knuckle of her right hand between the index and ring fingers.

Defensive wound…were there two shots or did the bullet go through my hand first?

She couldn't lift the hand to study it more as she would have any other case, and somehow that little detail caused a crack in her emotional wall and she started to cry. She lifted her hand to dry her tears, but her spirit-face was dry.

I guess real tears belong to the living.

An empty hole opened inside her as reality set in with a vengeance, racking her spirit every bit as hard as it would have when she was alive.

She didn't want to consider the idea of her death, but if she gave up, she thought she might truly disappear; then where would she be? Solving murders and putting away the bad guys were what she lived for. If the forces-that-be were going to let her continue doing that after her death, she wasn't about to kick her gift horse in the teeth.

She mimicked taking a long slow breath, picked up the pieces of the shattered emotional wall, and caged her feelings so she could continue. She moved to the single wound on her forehead. It wasn't round as most bullet wounds, making it hard to determine the caliber.

No visible GSR…the shooter had to be more than eighteen inches away.

She finished her examination and turned away, walking the hundred and fifty feet or so through the wooded area and fell to her knees beside the highway before she burst into tears again. This time she stayed like that for a half hour or more before she climbed to her feet and started walking. At first it was all she could do to put one foot in front of the other, but time and distance helped, and her mind turned back to solving the crime.

She still had more questions than answers.

Why can't I remember anything?

She knew the scene was staged to look like a rape and body dump, which meant the killer was most likely, someone she knew and probably trusted. Maybe even someone she loved or had once loved.

But who?

My fiancé, Frank...or...Wayne...

Oh God Lacy? I have to know if it was Wayne. I won't let Lacy live with a murderer, damn it!

The rising sun painted the sky with a subtle orange glow, behind the trees, showing her which way was east. She walked north a half mile before she came across a mile marker. The sign told her she was twenty miles north of Auburn on Highway 49. If she kept heading north, she'd end up in Grass Valley, but that meant this was Nevada County. She would probably find more answers in her own jurisdiction. Besides, home was in the other direction.

She crossed the highway and walked south as the sun rose over the trees. One good thing about being dead was that her legs never got tired. Walking, running, it didn't matter. Her legs felt as fresh as they did when she first woke up. Still the time it took to walk bothered her and she tried a few crazy things just to see what would happen. She walked down the middle of the highway and tried to grab on as a truck passed right through her. She didn't feel a thing. There was literally nothing for her to grab but air. Several cars and even a tour bus passed through her before she gave up on that idea and tried to will herself into town.

Lot of good that did her. She found out she could feel pain if she tried hard enough. Her head hurt for an hour after concentrating so hard it felt like her eyeballs had turned backwards in their sockets.

Running was the fastest mode of travel she had available. Since she could sprint all the way, it only took another hour before she was jogging up the steps to the Auburn Justice Center on Richardson Drive. The closed door offered no resistance as she put her hand on the metal bar to push it open. She went through the metal instead, throwing her off balance as she stumbled head-first through the thick glass door, coming out on the other side. With nothing to grasp or halt her progress she fell, shoving her hands through the cement floor. She screamed as the fear of being buried alive shook her spirit to the core and before she knew it she was flying backward through the door where she landed on her ass. This time the concrete steps held under her. She noted her fear returning a half second before she landed.

Maybe I can use that.

She looked around finding no one to witness her fall, so she got up and walked through the glass door. She continued beyond the front desk and down the long hallway to the broom closet they called her office. It was the third door on the left, next to Jason's. He was the other investigator assigned to the Auburn office. She headed straight for her desk, tried to sit down, and fell through the chair, landing hard on the tan adobe tiles below, as fear halted her from going through the stone. It didn't hurt, but her face still felt hot with embarrassment as she picked herself up and tried again, this time accessing the intense emotion at chair level, so she could sit. Luckily the chair was pulled out enough, so her desk didn't cut through her spirit form. The fear trick only stopped her from falling. It didn't let her move the chair or anything else.

She eyed the monitor as her fingers sank through the desktop to the keyboard on a tray below and she managed to set her fingers on the keys.

Damn.

Her fingers sank into the keyboard as she tried to type. She tried focusing her mind, adding a bit of fear into the mix, but that only gave her another headache. She got up and walked around the station, looking to see if there were any other ghosts around. No one seemed to notice her or even look her way, so she couldn't tell one way or the other.

What if no one can hear me?

Am I doomed to walk the earth surrounded by people who can't see or hear me?

Lizzy went back to her desk. She tried everything she could think of, including walking through a couple of people to get their attention, but nothing seemed to work. She couldn't even open the musty old yellow pages, because her fingers passed through the phone book instead of letting them do the walking like the old ads used to say. Desperate, she even tried sticking her face into the pages, but the words all jumbled together in a blur. It was like trying to read a page that someone had printed over the fonts a hundred times.

She stood and looked up shaking her fist in the air as she yelled, "Why didn't you just send me to hell? I obviously can't do anything here!"

There were no bright lights or demons sent to drag her away, so she stomped out of the sheriff's office and headed home. Better to surround herself with people who loved her than strangers, even if no one knows she's there.

Lizzy lived on the outskirts of Auburn in a small cottage-style apartment she shared with Frank and her ten-year-old daughter.

It took Lizzy ten minutes to run home. Not bad, seeing that it usually took almost twenty by car.

Her hand passed through the doorknob as she reached out to turn the handle to her apartment, before she threw her hands up and just walked through the door. She wondered about her father and uncle then.

Why aren't they here to help me?

Cancer had cut her uncle's life short, but at least he'd gotten to see Lizzy become a cop. He was like a father to her after her dad died. Her uncle had been on the force as well, retiring after forty years of service. He'd been gone eight years now, but she still missed him a lot. He never had a lot of time to spend with her, but somehow he found ways to help her get through every scrape she'd gotten into.

Thoughts of him brought home the memory of her daughter. She was born two years before he passed. How was she going to explain to her daughter that she was dead?

I have to figure out how to talk to the living, for Lacy's sake.

Lizzy marched into the kitchen. Her hand passed through the handle of the refrigerator. "Damn it. I hate this." She stuck her head through the door and tried to grab a beer. "Damn it. Am I already in hell or what? I can't even get a beer!" She was going to give whoever was in charge down here a piece of her mind—just as soon as she found the imbecile who orchestrated this mess, which had better be soon because she was on the edge of losing her mind.

Pissed and alone, Lizzy marched down the hallway to her desk in the den. The first thing she noticed was the mess of scattered case files and papers. That was pretty much how she left it most days, but for some reason she couldn't remember the last case she'd been working on.

She cursed again as she tried to thumb open one of the files and caught only air.

Leaning forward, her eyes locked on the only open file, dead center of the mess. She remembered it now. It was a special cold case she'd been browsing through. It was her dad's murder. Her uncle knew the lead detective on the twenty-five-year-old case, so he'd made her a copy. There had been three rape-murders, with the bodies dumped along Highway 49, before her dad was shot. Same MO as her murder. She thought maybe her dad had come across a lead and confronted the killer.

She wondered then if maybe she had read her crime scene wrong. Maybe her mind skipped over some of the signs to keep her from admitting she'd been violated.

Her hand flew to her mouth. "Oh God." Below was the photo of a young woman posed in the same way her body had been left. She read the report, which told how all three women were raped and killed elsewhere, and then their bodies were put on display. The only suspect they could nail down on the case was a twenty-eight-year-old truck driver, but he had an alibi for one of the murders. Her dad had circled that case and wrote "Gold" above it. It was a place to start, but not much. She didn't remember anything about it.

Gold what?

Gold coins…nuggets? Hell, I live in gold country…Well I used to live here, damn it, and I sure as hell died here.

Maybe she could track down all the old suspects. She knew alibis had a way of falling apart over time.

Girlfriends and wives become exes eager to spill the beans on the worthless bums who left them for younger women, especially if gold is involved.

Lizzy found the photo of the truck driver at the bottom of the report.

He'd be in his fifties now.

She finished reading the opened pages and tried again to peek below—to no effect. She stretched and yawned. She looked to the window. It was getting dark. She'd spent most of the day and only had one sketchy lead to go on. She yawned again. It didn't have the same effect that it had before, but she straightened up and headed for her bedroom just the same.

The master bedroom door was half open at the end of the hall. Not bothering to step around it, she plunged right through and stopped short at the edge of her bed. Blankets and pillows were strewn all over the floor. The top and bottom sheets were missing, and there was a red spot the size of a cantaloupe on her side of the mattress where her head would have been.

Just then she heard the front door open and close. She ran to the closet to hide, forgetting that no one could see her ghostly form. She heard a soft rumble like someone was dragging something across the laminate wood flooring down the hallway toward her. Remembering at last that nothing could hurt her, she stepped out of the closet just as her fiancé walked in dragging a carpet cleaner with an upholstery attachment.

Lizzy lost it.

She stormed through the closet doors "Frank, you freakin' SOB, you shot me in my own bed! How could you?"

Frank dropped the carpet cleaner. "Lizzy is that you? Where the hell have you been?"

"You oughta know. My body's right where you left it in a ditch along Highway Forty—" "Lizzy froze as her brain forged a tiny tunnel through the anger to realize that Frank had actually heard her speak. It made sense though. How was she supposed to haunt her killer the rest of his days if he couldn't hear her?

Frank stomped around the room opening the closet and bathroom doors looking for her. "Come on out now, Lizzy. This isn't another one of your crazy sex games is it? I've been worried sick about you."

Lizzy marched up behind him and shouted, "Crazy sex games! Crazy sex games! Frank, I'm a cop remember. I caught you red-handed trying to get rid of the blood stain where you shot me."

Frank turned around, staring right through Lizzy. "Come on out, Lizzy. I don't want to play this game anymore."

"I'm right here, Frank, and I'm not playing. You can't see me because I'm dead. You shot me in the head remember?"

"What the hell are you talking about? I didn't shoot you," Frank replied.

"Duh Frank. That's my blood over there on the bed. Isn't that why you're dragging around a rented carpet cleaner? It won't work by the way. When they luminol the bed, they'll find that spot and then they'll tear the mattress apart looking for a viable sample to compare with my DNA."

"That's not blood, Lizzy. It's wine. I had a nice romantic evening planned for us last night. I got pissed when you didn't show up and threw a pillow at your empty headboard. It knocked over the red wine on your nightstand. Now come on out, where I can see you."

"I'm standing right in front of you, Frank. I told you, I'm dead. My body was dumped out along Highway 49 about halfway to Grass Valley."

His face paled as he reached toward her voice in the empty air. "If you're dead, then how are you talking to me?"

"I haven't the foggiest. No one else can hear me, or see me for that matter. I woke up this morning in a ditch. I got up, but my body didn't. I've spent the day walking through walls and screaming at the top of my lungs, but no one has heard me—except you. Are you sure you didn't kill me? I had a perfectly good explanation all worked out; now I have to figure out why you're the only one who can hear me."

Tears rolled down Frank's cheeks as he stumbled to his side of the bed and snatched the phone from its charger. "If you're really dead I've got to call the police and tell them where you're at."

"That's a good idea, but—. Stop! Put the phone down Frank. You can't call them from here. They'll arrest you and stick a needle in your arm."

"But you know I didn't kill you."

"Think about it, Frank. How are you going to explain how you know where I'm at?"

"You told me where to find you."

"Yes, but they can't hear me. They'll think you're trying to plead an insanity case. They'll throw the book at you. I'm a cop, or I was. Cops take it personally when one of their own gets killed."

"What are we going to do?" Frank asked.

"I haven't got a clue, but you can't tell them where I'm at unless you're ready to die."

KNOCK, KNOCK, KNOCK. Someone pounded on the door.

Frank stood up and headed down the hall to answer it.

"Wait a minute, Frank. Let me ghost through the door and see who's out there before you answer it. I don't know who killed me or why, but I think it has something to do with an old case my father handled when he was lead detective. If my killer knows I've been looking into the case, then he might know where I live too."

"Be careful, Lizzy."

"I'm dead, Frank. What are they going to do, kill me again? Just cool your jets while I go have a look."

Lizzy stuck her head through the door. "It's okay, Frank. It's just my partner, Jason."

Jason had just lifted his fist to pound the spot where Lizzy's face poked through the door, then stopped, fist dropping to his side.

"Lizzy, thank God, you're home. What happened to—"

Lizzy stopped, face still poking out through the door. It was dark outside. The light over her door had burned out a week ago, but she kept forgetting to let Frank know, so it hadn't been changed. Lizzy could have changed it herself, but every time she cursed the darkness she'd ask herself, what's the use of having Frank around if I don't let him change a few light bulbs? Then, of course, her mind would drift back to whatever case she was working on and the thought of telling Frank the light was out would drift into that cluttered corner of her mind where the things in her personal life lay all but forgotten.

Able to see as clearly in the dark now as she had in daylight, Lizzy watched Jason turn three shades lighter. He was a healthy black man in his late twenties with an athletic body, short dark hair, a neatly trimmed moustache and a beard that circled his lips, connecting to his sideburns at mid-jaw line. Lizzy and he had had a fling after her divorce, but it never got serious. She wouldn't let it. They had to work together, so she ended it quickly before it had time to go anywhere.

At the moment, Jason's mouth was hanging wide open. "Hu…How are you doing that?" His voice had climbed an octave higher.

Realizing he could see her, Lizzy popped back inside and looked herself over. "Frank, get your butt in here and open the door. Jason saw me. Why can't you?" She stepped back a few paces to the couch and remembering her fear trick she sat while Frank marched down the hallway shaking his head as he looked this way and that. He opened the door and stood aside.

Jason stomped inside. "Where's Lizzy? I could have sworn I saw her through the door, but she glowed like one of those Halloween light sticks."

"I'm over here Jason. Can't you see me?

Both men turned toward her voice, but their gazes bypassed her moving on into the kitchen and then back.

"What the hell is going on here Lizzy? First you blow off your shift. The captain is pissed by the way, and now you're hiding behind the couch. Did Frank hit you?" Jason grabbed Frank's collar and started to twist it in his fist.

"Jason! Stop it right now. I'm not hiding. I'm dead. I'm sitting on the couch right now, but you saw me earlier… didn't you?"

Jason let go of Frank's shirt and the two men backed away from each other, heads turned toward the couch, but some-how Lizzy knew they still couldn't see her.

"Do me a favor, guys, turn out all the lights in here, and then come back."

Frank got the lights in the den and hallway while Jason killed the lights in the kitchen, ending with the lamp in the living room next to Lizzy.

She looked at her hands and noted the soft glow and almost see through image, like an imperfect reflection from a dark window.

"Lizzy, is that really you?" Jason asked.

"You know how I kind of step out of my body when I'm trying to solve a case. Well it looks like I really did it this time. All I had to do was die first."

Frank came up beside her and tried to take her hand, but his hand passed right through hers, so she just let her hand rest in the place where he laid his.

"How did you know about turning out the lights?" he asked.

"I saw it in a movie once, only the guy wasn't really dead."

Jason went down on one knee in front of Lizzy. "How sure are you that you're dead?"

Frank patted the air above her hand as a spark of hope lit his eyes.

"There's a bullet hole in my head. I'm pretty sure I'm dead, guys. My body is out along Highway 49, but it's across the county line, so we'll have figure out how to get my body without either of you being cuffed and booked for murder."

Jason stood up, his hand playing with his beard like he always did when he was thinking out loud. "Where's your cell phone, Lizzy?"

"How the hell should I know? It might be out by my body, it might not. My hands go right through everything I touch."

"I got your phone, Lizzy," Frank replied. "I grabbed it by mistake the other night."

"Great, that'll work." Jason said. "We can drop it out by your body and then we'll come back and file a missing person's report."

"Good thinking, partner. Let's go."

Lizzy followed the other two out to Jason's car, a 1968 GTO, red with black stripes. Lizzy slid through the right door to the back seat. She'd hadn't forgotten about falling through her chair at work earlier that morning, so she made sure her body stopped at the back seat where it was supposed to be and sat normally.

I think I'm getting the hang of this ghost thing.

Jason got behind the wheel and Frank rode shotgun. A small fear crept into Lizzy's mind as Jason started the car.

I hope I don't end up flat on my ass on the pavement when he guns it.

Thankfully, her ghost body stayed in the car as they drove out along Highway 49 to the spot Lizzy had marked in her mind. There was a dead pine surrounded by sorrel and a sapling growing in its shadow not far from where she'd left her body.

Frank and Jason both stumbled, trying to follow Lizzy in the dark. Jason had a flashlight, but every time he turned it on its pale light bled the image of Lizzy's ghost from the scene making it hard to follow her.

Lizzy marched forward to the clearing where she'd left her body, but her breath caught in her ghostly throat when they found the spot. "It's gone. My body is gone! It was right here, I swear."

Lizzy squatted over the impressions in the soft detritus covered soil.

"Are you sure?" Jason asked. "I can't see a thing out here. Let me turn on a light."

"Thanks, partner, but I can see just fine." Being able to see in the dark was about the only cool thing about being dead. Well that and the whole walking through walls bit, but sometimes that was just as frustrating as it was cool. When she was alive, Lizzy couldn't see a thing once the lights went out. She took her time now studying the scene. There were boot marks and a long cylinder-shaped pattern probably from a body bag next to where she had lain. There were also four long wheel trails from a stretcher, leading back to the highway.

Lizzy was about to stand up and announce that the cops had already come when flood lights from three SUVs filled the clearing.

A loud amplified voice rang through the trees. "Nevada County Sheriff's Department... Drop your weapons and freeze."

Frank's hands shot in the air as he held his breath trying not to move.

Lizzy moved unseen behind him and whispered, "Take a breath, Frank. I don't think he meant for you to stop breathing."

Jason snatched his badge from the clip on his belt and stepped forward holding it up in his right hand. "Hold on, guys. I'm a cop."

The hefty-looking man, with the megaphone held up to his handlebar moustache, stepped into the light as the clicks of three rifles being cocked silenced all voices. "Lay all your weapons on the ground in front of you and take two steps back," the sheriff blared.

Tiny red lights reflected off Jason's chest as he slowly raised his hands. Then using only his thumb and forefinger he removed the gun from his shoulder holster and flung it about ten feet away. Then he pulled up his pant leg and did the same with his back-up piece before taking two extra-long steps away from his weapons. Lizzy couldn't blame him. The whole racial profiling thing was no joke. They had partnered up on several big cases. Lizzy had seen firsthand how differently a black man was treated, even by his fellow officers.

The megaphone blared again. "Now, both of you, on the ground, faces down, with your arms stretched over your heads."

Frank and Jason did as they were told as two of the deputies lowered their weapons and walked out in front of their vehicles. Cuffs in hand, they both knelt down over the men, pulling each arm down and behind them as they secured their wrists in the metal bracelets.

The Sheriff lowered his bullhorn and came forward when the two deputies helped Frank and Jason to their feet. He stooped down and picked up Jason's badge from where it had fallen in the dirt and opened the fold.

"I'm sorry to detain you like this, Detective... Branson is it." He flashed his light from the photo next to the badge to Jason's face and back. "—but one cop's been shot already out here. I need to have a few questions answered before I turn you loose."

Frank turned his head looking off in the direction where Lizzy last spoke to him.

"Is there someone else out here with you two?" The sheriff asked.

Lizzy caught Frank's partial nod as Jason shook his head emphatically; then Frank just stopped and stood still.

The sheriff turned his head to the man behind him. "Check the area. Detective Branson here was a little too quick with his answer, and his partner had a different opinion..." The Sheriff nodded and the deputy holding Frank searched his pockets and fished out Frank's wallet.

"Frank Winslow." The deputy answered.

"Thanks, Jimmy. Now while were a waitin' for them to find whoever else you got out here with ya. Why don't you tell me why you're here?"

"Don't say a word, Frank. Let Jason do the talking," Lizzy whispered.

Frank hung his head, a look of doom clearly written all over his face. He was the worst liar in the world. His face betrayed his true feelings every time. It was why Lizzy had fallen for him. Her ex was too good at lying and she had had her fill of liars, especially with her job.

Jason responded quickly. "We're looking for my partner. Elizabeth Turner. She's got GPS on her phone, so I traced it out here. I went looking for her when she missed her shift today."

"I see and what does Frank Winslow have to do with this?" The sheriff questioned.

"He's Lizzy's fiancé. We found her phone out there in the woods. You said an officer had been shot out here? It wasn't Lizzy, was it?"

The deputy came back shrugging his shoulders and shaking his head as the sheriff acknowledged him with a look. He nodded at the two deputies that held Frank and Jason and they unlocked their cuffs.

"I'll need that cell phone you found, so our forensic boys can sort this thing out. I'm releasing you for the moment, but you're both still suspects. You'll have to follow us down to the office in Nevada City to make your statements." He put a hand on Jason's shoulder.

"Now to answer your last question. Yes, detective, your partner was shot, but she's not dead. A couple of hikers found her three hours ago. The ME found a pulse, so she's at Sierra Nevada Memorial. Well go right past it on the way to the station, and you should be able to look in on her after you've made your statements."

Lizzy stood still. The shock of the sheriff's last words left her emotions in a tangled knot. She'd just gotten used to the idea of being dead. Now that she knew she wasn't, an intense longing deep inside pulled her toward her body.

She woodenly followed Frank and Jason to the GTO, sliding into the back through the seats as before. Jason drove. It was his car after all.

Frank tapped incessantly on the dash, anxious to get the interview over. Lizzy knew he wanted to go see her body as badly as she did, but they had to deal with the sheriff first.

The staccato of Frank's tapping ate into Lizzy's thoughts like a colony of ants on a crumb left from a picnic.

"Stop it, Frank. You're driving me crazy!"

Her voice was a trigger that broke the icy chill that had kept everyone from talking. Both Frank and Jason spoke at once, making it impossible to understand either one.

Frank closed his mouth first and waited with his jaws clenched while Jason continued, "This hick sheriff is wasting our time. I'm going to ditch him and head to the hospital first. We've got to get you back into your body before you're dead for real."

Frank's voice dropped to a gravelly timber. "The sheriff will know where we're going. He'll drag us back to the station in cuffs."

"Chill out both of you," Lizzy yelled. "Jason, follow the sheriff. Frank's right. Besides, the sheriff's office isn't that far from the hospital. I can run there almost as fast as you can drive…through town anyway."

If I don't die between now and then.

"Are you sure, Lizzy? If you die on me, I'll never forgive you." Jason said.

"If we don't get this sheriff off our backs, we'll never figure out who tried to kill me or why. That's more important to me."

Frank's face turned a shade or two whiter. But he held the grimace, as if his face was carved in stone. It was one of the things Lizzy loved about him. He would do the right thing. Always.

I can't believe I suspected him of shooting me.

Lizzy saw the hospital sign as they pulled into town. "I'm just going to step out here, boys," she said as Jason stopped at a red light.

Frank opened the car door a crack and leaned forward, but Lizzy just stood up, her head going through the roof as her feet sank to the road beneath.

When Jason drove forward, her essence drifted through the trunk, leaving her standing in the middle of the road. She waved, even though they couldn't see her under the bright street lights.

Lizzy stretched her senses out, trying to feel a connection to her body as she ran the four and a half blocks to the hospital. As far as she could tell, there wasn't a connection.

Lizzy walked into the emergency room entrance and started poking her head into each curtained off room. She breathed in the sterile atmosphere as an empty IV bag set off an alarm. She kept on moving down the curtained off rooms, praying her body wasn't already down in the morgue. The last room at the end of the hallway yielded a female patient with tubes and wires covering her features.

That couldn't be me.

The plastic bracelet on her wrist said different. Lizzy laid down on the bed letting her spirit pass through the tubes to merge with her body. She lay there for some time, hoping to feel something, some sign of connection to her body but nothing changed. She sat up, leaving her physical form connected to the machines. She got off the table and walked around the bed just as her ex-husband showed up.

How did he know I was here?

"Are you the one who shot me, Wayne?"

He didn't say word as he moved toward the machines and pulled the plugs from the wall.

Alarms and bells blared through the room as Lizzy screamed, "Stop! Stop!"

Wayne walked right through her body without seeing or feeling her. He barred the door as nurses tried to get in.

Lizzy tried to pull him from behind, but she was only a spirit. Her hands passed through him like the empty hot air she always said he was full of.

The heart monitor slowed in its rhythm until it made a long, solid squeal. Lizzy ran to her body and tried to jump in, willing her heart to start beating again. Time seemed to pass like cold honey dripping from a hive. A couple of seconds passed as a lone blip registered on the heart monitor. And then another and another until the rhythm developed into a normal pattern. By the time Lizzy looked up again, several nurses were reconnecting the lines. On the floor, two uniformed security guards held Wayne down as he kicked and fought against them, yelling, "You're not going to keep her on that damn machine for months on end. I won't let my daughter go through the hell I did with my mom!"

"Secure his wrists and get him out of here," the heavyset guard replied.

The thinner, taller guard zip tied Wayne's wrists together as two others came in and helped drag Wayne out of the room. He continued to yell fighting against the guards and cuffs that held him.

Lizzy sat up, but her body remained flat on the hospital bed. She got up and watched as one female and three male guards marched Wayne down the hall with his hands secured behind his back.

She remembered one time he'd broken down in front of her. His mother was in a car accident that had left her brain dead, but Wayne's sister, refused to pull the plug. Their mother lasted three whole months before even the machines couldn't keep her alive. Those three months killed the man she married and left a self-absorbed asshole in his place.

Nurses filtered out through her spirit to tend to other patients. Her heart was beating on its own now.

At least that's a good sign.

She didn't know the extent of her injuries. She prayed the bullet hadn't damaged her brain.

The last nurse finished checking everything, then turned the lights down low and left the room, closing the door behind her.

Lizzy tried once again to reconnect to her body, letting her spirit meld with her flesh. Time slowed to a crawl. It seemed like she'd almost made a connection, but it was like trying to catch the wind. Each time she felt the resistance against her spiritual hand, the bond slipped from her grasp like water leaking through the tiny cracks between her fingers.

An hour passed with no progress, but it gave her time to think. She wondered why only Frank and Jason could see her when Wayne couldn't. She knew Frank and Jason both loved her in their own ways, and the only person Wayne ever loved was himself. Maybe he loved Lacy, but no one else.

Love…Fear…I wonder if emotions have something to do with it.

The idea seemed to slip from her mind. It was getting harder to think.

Digging for answers was like mining for gold.

Gold…Gold…

Lizzy's mind flashed to an image of a fat man on a lounger, but his image faded into a misty fog before she could focus on it. Another hour went by and her mind returned to her problem of putting herself back together. Her spirit form seemed only to respond to emotions. Fear kept her from sinking into the earth and love let her communicate. But what emotion did she need to make herself whole?

Maybe…

The door opened, and the idea that had floated into her mind before, drifted back into the forefront of her memory. Bright lights from the hall flashed in her eyes, but her spirit had no trouble seeing the heavyset man who walked in. He was dressed in a tan security uniform like the ones who took Wayne into custody, only Lizzy recognized him instantly. He was the man from the lounger. Her gaze flashed to the nametag on his breast pocket. It read Henry Gold.

Gold.

Henry walked up beside Lizzy's bed, staring right at her, but she knew he was staring at her sleeping body, because he put his hand on her side and shook her to see if she'd wake up.

GOLD!

The fog in her mind cleared as she remembered knocking on Henry Gold's door and then walking around back. He was sitting in a lounger when she confronted him about his whereabouts on the day her dad was killed. He never answered. He just pulled a gun from under the seat cushion and shot at her and—

She saw Henry pull out a syringe half-filled with green liquid.

Oh God stop him!

He grabbed the IV tube and—

The door banged opened as Lacy walked in followed by Lizzy's mom.

"Who are you?" Lacy asked.

"Mom call security. This is the guy who shot me!"

"Lizzy? Is that you?" How—

Henry hid the needle behind his back and ran for the door knocking Lizzy's mom to the floor.

Lizzy, still in spirit form, sprinted after him through her daughter and mom's legs and out into the hall as Henry ran for the elevator. Ten steps ahead of him the double doors of the elevator slid open. Jason stepped out followed by Frank.

"Stop him, Jason! He's the one who shot me."

Henry slammed into Jason before he could pull his gun and the two men wrestled on the floor. Then Frank grabbed a metal bedpan from a cart and bashed the older man in the head. Henry stopped fighting long enough for Jason to grab his cuffs and slap them on Henry's wrists.

Lizzy rushed up to give Frank a hug, but her arms passed right through him. She turned around and headed back to her room. Her mom had gotten back to her feet and was holding Lacy.

Lizzy crawled back up on the hospital bed determined to put herself back together. If love was the glue that made her whole, she had all she needed.

Frank, Jason, her mom, and Lacy all had hearts of gold; they loved her very much.

Lizzy channeled all of that love, letting it infuse her, but it wasn't enough. She knew the key to this solution was tied to her emotions. She had the love of family and friends.

Maybe…maybe.

She had blamed herself for her divorce…For not seeing through Wayne's lies…For spending too much time away from Lacy and Frank.

Maybe I need to forgive myself…learn to love myself again.

She let all those thoughts find purchase as she let go of her guilt. Then she opened her heart and let herself in. She found the love she needed to make herself whole. It wasn't the kind of self-love that Wayne had. It wasn't egotistical love.

Then she opened her eyes.

The bright lights from the hallway blinded her momentarily, but as her vision cleared she welcomed the sight of her loved ones surrounding her bed. She had a killer headache and her hand hurt too, but for the first time in her life she welcomed the pain as well.

NANER

Dennis Grayson

I THINK. THEREFORE, I AM. I am a Naner. One of billions upon billions of Naners cast out unto the cosmos by They-Who-Propagate. I am but a speck. No…less than a speck. Infinitesimal, yet I am a life-starter. Or, I will be a life-starter. I have yet to make planetfall and carry out my Prime Directive.

Like my facsimile Naners, I was grown and shaped as a six-dimensional fractal-crystallite, utilizing all eight hundred and forty-one lattices. Development and refinement took place within a sterile micro-vacuum aboard a vessel orbiting far out on the edge of the home planetary system of They-Who-Propagate. Half a planet rotation ago, we Naners were evaluated as being properly cured and fully matured. It was then that our growth-lab was disassembled by pre-programmed, self-euthanizing, gobbler nanobots, and all Naners were freed to disperse.

Now, Naners are at the beginning of our mission—to start life throughout the Universe again and again to ensure there shall always be a species akin to They-Who-Propagate.

We scatter! A starwind impels us.

～

Increased gravity pulls at me. It comes from a mass of swirling stars. A galaxy. I have drifted past hundreds of thousands of galaxies for over one billion planet orbits of the They-Who-Propagate star system. This one has captured me. I look forward to finding out if I will make planetfall or pass through it; much like a subatomic particle penetrates a molecule.

∿

Continuing to travel inward toward the center of this galaxial mass, I pass through two of its spiral arms and many supernova remnant loops. None of these compel me to alter course. My inertia defeats their pull and propels me toward a smaller gas bubble where a target of star clusters would seem to be my destination. Another thousand planet orbits and I should be able to make a determination if this is a suitable choice for planetfall.

∿

This small bubble is an omen. Naners do not believe in omens, but They-Who-Propagate do, and Naners learned from them. The bubble is configured much like a biological cell. I have passed through the almost perfectly circular perimeter, and just off dead-center is a denser cluster of stars, very much resembling the nuclei of a cell. Yes, They-Who-Propagate would consider this a good portent.

I shall close distance with the target.

∿

Time to make an assessment. Before me lies a star system of many planets and planetoids. The question before me is: can any of them support life? If yes, then I need only use .003

milli-electron volts of energy to alter my course by one-mil-lionth of a degree to assure planetfall. If not, I must use a slightly larger energy release to change my vector in order to bypass this system and journey on, perhaps to another star system or even another galaxy. I must be careful since my discharge force will be limited to an attosecond and I must choose the azimuth exactly.

To gather information, I shall send out a single antipro-ton ping. It will take sixty-seven planet orbits to receive my back-ping.

~

Data from the ping indicates the star system of interest has a span of three planetary orbit rings with the potential of sustaining life. All have metal cores. Surely, one of them holds H_2O.

Altering course.

~

I now drift though the cloud of comets surrounding my target star system. It lies out beyond the last of the gas giant planets. A second ping confirms that the world in the third orbit around this star contains vast quantities of H_2O on its surface. Also, the planet is volcanically active, thus capable of mixing together an abundant fusion of elements.

~

Planetfall! I, Naner, now find myself in a sea full of miner-als. Volcanic vents spew gaseous bubbles up from the bottom of the ocean. I ride such a bubble as it glides past simple mol-ecules, which can bind and form a more complex chemical structure. I utilize minute sparks to encourage molecules to weld and adhere to the surface of the bubble.

My success rate is nearly seventy percent. Methane and hydrocarbons now float in a liquid medium, staged for the next phase.

～

Riding 1,214,657,817.0005 orbits of this planet about its star, I find my efforts successful despite repeated near-extinction episodes triggered by space debris striking this world and ongoing shifts of atmospheric content. I must now induce these more intricate molecules to self-organize into self-nurturing and self-protecting clusters. These will then need to construct membranes around themselves in order to separate their potential life processes from toxic non-living matter.

～

Proto-cells are now capable of electrostatic interactions. Not life, but I sense I am but a step away.

～

Rafts of bluish bacteria float in and on the seas of this world. They capture the energy of starlight. They process chemicals and expel waste in the form of oxygen. They are cells. They are life.

～

Floating at the very boundary between water and land, I am in a swampy environment where low-salinity H_2O flows into and mixes with a large body of brackish water. Vegetation, which survives growing in the water and on the mounds of mud rising up into the atmosphere, carpets the topography. For 3,500,000,012 planetary orbits of this star I have waited as life became ever more complex. Except for plants, all other life has been limited to existing in seas and lakes. It is time for animal life to move to land.

I have found a creature living near the mud humps that I will encourage to cross over. It has a proto-backbone and uses four appendages to drag itself along the bottom of the shallow pool, lured along by food. In its mouth, rows of spike-like teeth declare it to be a carnivore.

After exerting sufficient force and breaking through the surface tension of the H_2O, I float to a mud hump. As I do so, I periodically trigger a spark, which attracts the attention of the creature. It continues to stalk me as I roll onto the land. We play this game for a quarter of a planet rotation. Eventually its hunger pulls it back to the water.

I carry on this game with this creature for hundreds of planetary orbits. Eventually, the beast makes its way to land without prompting. Soon, others join it.

Success!

~

It has taken 493,498,620 planetary orbits for land life to diversify. There are several species which demonstrate potential to develop into beings resembling They-Who-Propagate. Currently, they live in forest canopies and grasslands. They are easy prey for predators. I must correct this situation.

I engage these primitive creatures with sustained games over tens of thousands of orbits of this planet, concentrating my efforts on the males of the species. They provide food for the females and their young. They scavenge predator kills and must quickly and efficiently carry the food to safe locations. To motivate the primitives, I move the predators' food sources farther away from the secure zones of the primitives. I lure the prey by sparking as I ride the air currents. Where they go, the carnivores follow. Now the primitives are forced to travel afar to gather meat, and must figure out how to bear it back to their families. They accomplish this by using only their arms to carry carrion while running erect on their legs. Repeated reinforcement of this activity results in permanent anatomical adjustments and bipedalism.

⁓

The time is opportune for me to finalize my mission on this world. My current journey has been difficult. I, Naner, have been ingested by a female biped, flowed through the interior of its body, and made my way to its brain. I then reconnoitered multiple locations where mirror neurons reside. These are capable of performing abstractions across a webbed cortical system. Satisfied that this organism is in optimal working condition, I make my way to a well-hidden, thin sheet-like structure of tissue capable of controlling the brain network.

Now I spark the tissue.

Success! It…she is self-aware. It will take many generations, but her offspring and their descendants will pass the spark forward as they develop knowledge, cultures, and civilizations.

Now I must wait. Wait until these beings acquire technologies capable of freeing themselves from the gravitational mass of this world. Only then will I be able to hitch a ride back into the open cosmos and once again drift on intergalactic superwinds to search for another planet in need of a life-starter.

I cannot help but wonder how long I shall have to wait? Eons?

It matters not. I shall be patient. This is my purpose.

I am Naner.

Faster Than Light

Stephen Prey

Saint Hope Hospital: ER Treatment Station, 4AM

JAMES BLAKE LEANED FORWARD on the treatment chair, both hands facing upward on the equipment tray standing before him. The triage nurse examined the grayish green skin of his palms and fingers for frostbite damage.

My hands and fingers feel less numb. Feeling returning in my arms. More pain.

The nurse lightly applied some medicated salve. "You're telling me that you simply woke up this morning with frostbite damage to your hands?"

"Yes."

"The centers of your palms seem the most injured, and the fingertips are slightly…what…" Her hazel eyes opened wide. "Your hands are starting to glow *greenish*. And now the skin's color, it's becoming normal pink. Mr. Blake, I don't understand. This should not be happening!"

My body feels tingly, like a Jacuzzi bath. "Is it that anti-pain salve you put on my hands?" *More feeling surging to my hands. Less pain. Wow. Never felt this before. Something new.*

"Mr. Blake, nothing I've done to your hands and fingers could have made your skin glow or spontaneously heal! Do you mind if I get my phone and take a video of this for the doctor?"

"Uh, okay with me."

She took off her gloves and reached into her scrubs pocket for her cell phone. "The rest of your hands' surfaces are rapidly changing." Although she hurried to document the phenomenon, her shoulders slumped, and she lowered her phone. "I was too slow. Your hands seem normal. Any pain?"

James gently flexed his fingers, curling them into a fist and snapping them open and closed a few times. Each time he made a stronger fist. A shiver coursed through his body. "No pain anywhere. Thank you."

"I did nothing. Were you near any low temperature pipes earlier this morning?"

"Nowhere really, I was just relaxing in bed. I dreamed a little. When I woke up, both of my hands felt numb from my wrist to my fingertips. My arms felt like they were on fire. So I wrapped them with two clean dishtowels and drove here. The rest you've seen."

"I'd like to have one of our doctors fully check your hands and maybe run some tests."

He began to recall some of his memories of last night's dream and asked himself if that special trip could be the cause of his injuries. He started to feel like he was walking into a trap. If the nurse called in any doctors, they might try to keep him here for further tests.

Need to get out of here–don't want to be someone's lab rat or be held for a psych eval. What happened to me? "Maybe later." *I do remember now.* "I need to go. Thank you."

"Mr. Blake, I really think you–"

"Sorry, no, I've got to get back to my…house, er, office. Again, thank you."

He rose off the chair, grabbed his wallet, along with his medical card. He then shook the hand of the nurse and hurried out of the room.

Need to get out of here. Get home. Check my bed. Did I really fly to…

~

Earlier that evening at home: about 12:30 am

James settled himself on his waterbed. For the last two years he had practiced a process of getting his body ready for spiritual wandering. To do so, he had put his health at risk by forcing his body into type 2 diabetes, a family trait that would otherwise have come on later in life. Having excess sugar in his system increased the speed into his trance-state. Also, once his body processed his system's surplus sugar, he would be pulled back from his investigative flights. The more calories in his system, the longer the trip lasted. He knew he was shortening his life. But he felt the discoveries and possible financial gain might be worth the hazards.

Lying flat on the waterbed, James felt the warmth relax his muscles as he closed his eyes. He started to reduce his breathing. He then focused on finding body positions on the mattress' surface where moving any part of his body would increase pain or be more uncomfortable.

~

I ate way too much food tonight. My blood sugar is spiking more quickly.

Eyelids feel heavy. Don't go to sleep. Focus on feeling weightless. Visualize the body as a hollow vessel. Relax!

Take slow deep breaths. Imagine filling the body with an orange fluid to be absorbed by any points of stress.

Slowly let out the breath and let the mass of the orange fluid flow out my mouth.

Take smaller breaths, search for any orange residue. Search my body. Look for any orange. Left calf. Orange. Relax. Relax. Relaaaax. Orange intensity is lighter. Relax, almost no color.

Still color, visualize the remaining points of orange...

Last of the orange is gone.

Slowly breathe out all remaining air in my body.

Draw in fresh air and envision filling my body with the green fluid of energy. Ensure all crevices are filled. Review–slowly–search. Take very slow shallow breaths.

Time to float.

Lift out of the body. Carefully float.

My astral body rises.

So slowly. A green cord links both my bodies at the belly button.

The deep emerald-green cord is almost two inches thick. I move around the room and house a bit, then up through the fireplace chimney.

~

James drifted up and out through the chimney vent and, as in prior flying launches, passed through the abandoned dove nest. This time he did not stop and think about having the flue cleaned. He had finally learned his lesson. If he started to think about something he saw along the way, he would get pulled back into his body or to that object of the thought. Sometimes he could re-launch a flight; however, most of the time he went to sleep and did not remember the chimney flue in need of maintenance.

James knew that keeping focus was the hardest skill to learn. His brain may be a linear processor, but it looked for any excuse to explore any distraction, and caused the flight to end up in unusual places. As a result, James's motto was: just think of where you want to go, and there you are! And keep focused.

Once free of the chimney, he stared up at the full moon—and he was above the moon's surface.

~

Fly over the Moon's surface.

The crater-pocked surface slides by. Pull back from the Moon's surface and head for its dark side.

Look out into the black void from behind the moon and remember where Saturn should be in the sky. Easy to see a brighter point of light in the sky. Focus! Saturn.

Must be a way out. Saturn is about a hand's width wide. Its light is nowhere as bright as the...too late. I'm back at the Moon. Damn! Saturn.

Approach the rings of the planet.

See a rock, and I'm next to it. Looks like broken rock. Black with tiny pockmarks. Lots of tiny dust and sand-sized grains floating all around it. Turning around, more of the same. Back to the rock. Grab for the rock and my hand passes right through it. There's a small moon off in the distance. It's so bright.

Soaring above the small moon's surface.

It is quite reflective. What's the surface like?

Almost on the surface. Re-orient my body to a standing position.

Something is moving this snow-like dust. Very subtle surface wind blowing. Not quickly. Just slowly shifting. Not sure what's causing it.

Shift to an outcropping to my left. Seems more solid. Looks like blue ice!

Still no interaction with the objects around me.

It would be nice to find a way to leave a footprint in the fine powder layer.

Hmmm, feeling something tingling throughout my body. So far, I've only had a floating, non-feeling tactile sense from within. Focus! My cord is glowing brighter. Feet feel a little cool down around my thermal socks, and they are glowing too. How can I be feeling anything?

Nah, this can't be happening. My feet settle upon the powdery surface and seem to be compressing and moving the surface particles. Focus!!

UP!

My body lifts above the surface and backs away a few feet.

Looking down. Wow! I see two slight depressions in the powder, where my feet had been.

My feet are glowing a little less than before. Wait, they're still glowing.

This is new!

Make a snowball. Looking at hands as they are glowing much brighter than my feet. Not wearing socks on my hands. FOCUS!

To the surface again. Stooping over to see if the powder moves by touching it. FOCUS!

At first, fingertips are passing through the powder. No change in the snow.

Focus more on the material below, hands flare brighter. The cord is also much brighter and seems a little thinner, not much change.

Hands glowing a bright emerald green now. The movement of my fingers through the powder disturbed the flakes.

I see shallow furrows in the snow where my moving fingers had just been.

More focus allows me to move more powder. Cup my right hand to scrape the surface snow into a mound about four inches high.

Try to compress the powder into a ball? FOCUS!

Hands are ablaze now. They reach for the pile and scoop it up.

Make a ball of it.

Nothing happens, the powder is still a powder.

If dry snow needs to warm up to make a snowball back on Earth–

~

PAIN!!!

As he snapped awake in his own bed, James's forearms throbbed and burned.

"What the hell?"

He tried to roll off his stomach and onto his back. He struggled to sit up and turn on the bedside lamp. His hands were slow to react, his fingers felt numb. His arms felt on fire from his wrists to his elbows.

The more he tried to work with his fingers, only increased the discomfort. So he tried to minimize their use. Still, he finally managed to twist the switch, turning on the light.

He glanced to the clock.

"Crap, it's only 3:17 in the morning."

In agony, he studied the ash-gray color of his skin—from mid-forearms to the tips of the fingers.

Got to get to the ER. This will not be a fun drive.

~

Three months later. Saint Hope Hospital: ER, 6:45AM

"How bad is the right foot, Doc?" James felt the meds deaden the crushing pain, now only feeling pressure below his calf. "Will I lose a toe or two?"

"That's a possibility. What happened?"

"I smashed my toe on…on a rock by my bed."

"A rock?"

James smiled to himself. *Made of iron and nickel. A small asteroid actually, from last night's flight!*

Scavenger Hunt

Lee Garrett

MY LIFE FLASHED BEFORE my eyes. I had no regrets as I exploded through the second story window, revolved in flight, and fell to the street in a glittering hail of broken glass. I hit feet first and released the tension from my legs so they buckled. I rolled to spread the impact, and the last of my momentum lifted me to my feet again—in time to see the campus shuttle bearing down on me.

Always something.

I wilted to the pavement and lay on my back.

The vehicle shot over me, tingling my skin with cyan blue radiance. My weight lessened with a descending-elevator feeling, and I drifted up a few inches off the pavement. The crystal song of the bus' hover field thrummed through me, leaving a shiver in my bones as it went on. Weight returned and I dropped to the pavement.

I tucked my legs and rocked back onto my shoulders. My palms went to either side of my head, pushing against the street as I kicked my legs forward. This flipped me into the air, onto my feet. The move was unnecessarily flashy, but what the hell, I'd already become a spectacle.

Cadets were stopped outside the Student Lounge. They stared as I brushed myself off. A few even clapped.

Gina Powers stood among them in a student's gold-and-black, formal, one-piece uniform. She smiled, her pink-dyed hair ruffled by a friendly wind. In place of the usual regulation boots, she wore a bright red pair made of raptor hide. Off-world imports, they were hideous and hideously expensive. Only having her father in charge of the school let her get away with snubbing the dress code—that, and the note from her podiatrist claiming she needed the boots for *therapeutic* purposes. She grinned as I came up to her. The drama over, the other students flowed around us toward various destinations.

"Ryuu, you sure know how to make an exit," she said.

"Wasn't my idea. I was *thrown* out that window."

I looked up and saw Frigg peering down with cool blue eyes, her blonde head poking past some jagged glass still in the frame. She cupped her mouth and yelled. "Sorry about that. I don't know who put that window right where I was throwing you. Landed on your feet; good thing you're part cat."

Gina laughed in my ear. "Do we want to know which part?"

I yelled up the wall, "Next time you want to practice throws, we do it at the gym."

Frigg frowned and shouted. "You're no fun."

"Tell me about it," Gina shouted up the wall at her. "This guy's idea of a hot date is free climbing a cliff face and glide-chuting down for a ten-mile cross-country run."

I widened my eyes to dramatize my sense of injury. "I thought we had fun. Besides, that part of the Sangre de

Cristo range is where the wilderness trials are usually held. We've seen it first hand. We're bound to do better than the rest of the class."

"Only reason I didn't kill you." Gina paused to whip pink hair out of her face as the wind changed. "I thought we were tackling snow; in skiing, I wouldn't have come in second place."

I held up a hand for silence, cocking my head to listen.

"What is it?" Gina asked.

I looked into the clear blue depths of the New Mexican sky and pointed. "Incoming."

Gina looked where I pointed. A blue-white star had appeared; the hover field of a lunar transport. There was an attenuated rumble. Moments later, I made out the silver needle that rode that blue star toward the nearby spaceport.

"First time seeing a landing?" Gina asked. "That can't be right. You've been here four years and the starport's only a few miles away."

"That's not it." I winced. "Something's wrong with its drive. Listen to the hum."

"What hum? No one but *you* have ever claimed to hear field inharmonics." She put a fist on her right hip. "I think you're just making it up."

The star went nova—a blinding wash of light—followed by the thunderclap of an explosion. Fragments of metal hailed, trailing black wiggles of smoke. It was fortunate the port lay outside the Santa Fe city limits; falling debris could otherwise have proven lethal.

Gina gasped in shock, eyes wide as the anime character she impersonated. "Oh…my…God."

A hush settled over the campus. Muscles knotted at the corners of my jaw. My eyes narrowed to a glower I'd inherited from generations of samurai warriors. I don't like it when Death wins. And this had been the second transport crash in a year. There would have been at least a dozen people per transport, people with families. I empathized with their pain, having lost my mother at an early age. Some wounds never heal, we just learn how to lock grief in a dark closet and keep going.

My wrist-comm chimed. Lifted toward my face, it displayed a prismatic dome set in a blue-steel band. The dome fanned intersecting planes of light that fused into a holo-field. A translucent icon faded in, a greenish, corpse-like face with a scar on the forehead and a flat head. The figure had bolts in the side of his neck like battery terminals. The monstrous face opened its mouth to speak, showing yellowed teeth and black gums.

"Fifteen-minute warning. You have Xeno-Archeology next."

I nodded to my personal AI. "Thanks, Frank."

The holograph growled and faded.

I looked over as Gina's wrist-comm activated. Her hologram, a guy duded up in tux and tails, was…*me!* His digital voice said, "Oh, precious flower of my heart, Xeno-Biology awaits your graceful indulgence."

"You made a smarmy *icon* out of me?"

"Sure, this way, I can always have you at my beck and call. C'mon, I'll walk you to class. It's on my way." Moving on, she smiled sweetly.

I high-voiced a fake, Gone-With-the-Wind southern accent, "Thank you, Ma'am. I'd be *ever* so grateful."

"You've been watching classic movies on late-night vid again," she said.

I thought of all the hours I'd spent cramming this last two weeks for finals. "Not lately."

We hadn't gotten far when Frigg caught up from behind, her arms going around our necks as she sandwiched between us. Locked in step, we continued past the huge bronze statue of Bryce McKnight, founder of the school. His eternal glare did little to quell us. Even the lunar transport had had only a transitory effect, though the underclassmen still pooled at various spots to discuss the matter in subdued tones. They'd harden up after receiving rigorous training or get washed out of the school's Off-World Careers Program.

Space is not a place for wimps.

We seniors were conditioned not to get distracted and unfocused by disaster. The work ahead had endless dangers to be taken in stride. Psychological tests had already weeded out students that were less than resilient, unable to compartmentalize their fear responses and act clear-headed in panic situations.

"You were leaving me behind!" Frigg wailed.

"So, what's your point?" I asked.

"Hi Frigg, what's new?" Gina jumped in.

"We got a guest speaker for class today, a scout captain, I hear. Oh, and I've been planning my graduation party. You guys are coming, right?"

"Don't you actually have to graduate first?" I climbed a short flight of stairs, taking them only one at a time since the girls were with me.

"What are you trying to say?" Frigg asked.

I shrugged. "I'd spend more time studying and less time planning celebrations if I were you. Didn't you just *barely* survive mid-terms?"

"Oh, groan of darkest despair, don't remind me."

The walkway took us between glass and steel buildings. We passed a circular basin and fountain, moving toward a butterscotch-adobe, three-story that had teal blue trim on the windows and royal blue clay tiles on the roof. The sign on the building said Richardson Hall. I angled for the main doors which had a Santé-Fe chic, long-horn skull hanging over the entrance.

Gina peeled off, continuing on with a goodbye wave.

Frigg stayed, having the same class I did. I opened the door for her, something she wouldn't have let any other guy do. I could get away with a lot since I'd grown up with her. We were more brother and sister than childhood friends— even though I'd stolen my first kiss from her when we were eleven. She'd often kicked my butt, mostly because I couldn't stand to hurt her. Growing up, it gave her an advantage she'd exploited shamelessly. Her Norwegian family had lived next to mine. She'd been named after the queen of Asgard. I could easily picture her waving a Viking sword around, giving off a blood-curdling scream.

Inside the building, air conditioning made my damp shirt cling to my back like an icy bandage. The floors were tiled in turquoise. The ochre walls were enlivened with color photos from several of the local Indian reservations. At the appropriate room number, we went in, taking adjoining seats near the windows. For a change, our teacher wasn't already in the room, waiting in his usual white suit, pastel handkerchief, and round glasses, capturing the light and letting it go in hypnotic rhythms.

The lady faculty members tended to sigh over him, and occasionally drool. Even a few female cadets flirted with him. I was less impressed. Sure, the guy was big, but my muscles didn't come from a machine in a gym. I earned them risking life and limb against vertical rock, surviving on the strength of my judgment, pushing my endurance in cross-country running. Kendo practice further honed my skills to a razor edge. The only reason my father let me come to an American school was my promise to train faithfully. I had kept up with my training—even in the hustle of approaching graduation. Dad claimed failure to follow through would shame my ancestors.

Me, I figure once you're dead, you have better things to do than mope around your descendants, living vicariously through them. Course, I might be wrong.

A murmur washed across the room as the door opened and Dr. Reginald Bolivar breezed in, striding to the lectern with a stranger behind. The visitor wore an X-Corps uniform, a polished copper body suit with a tarnish-green jacket and boots. The winged-star insignia on his shoulder patches sent a thrill trough me that surpassed getting tossed through the window. The spacer was thin and well over six feet, with a leathery, bronzed skin that had felt the warmth of a hundred suns. He moved with a rolling gait that seemed slow but covered ground quickly.

Bolivar took up his usual position in front of the class, draping himself over the lectern. "No class today," he drawled. "Senior class is being conscripted into service. This is Captain Tarique. You'll take instruction from him. Go back to your dorm and get your field gear, then report to the main gates for transportation and deployment."

Frigg thrust a hand into the air. "Excuse me, but what exactly will we be doing?"

The Captain answered without prompting from Bolivar. "Along with other volunteers, you will be combing the area outside of town where the ARIEL exploded. Eventually, all small debris will be gathered to a central location for inspection. For now, you'll be doing a preliminary sweep. Should you find human remains, drop a radio-marker and notify me at once by comm link. Make sure you bring trail rations and plenty of water."

A startled silence gripped the room.

"What are you waiting for?" Bolivar made shooing motions with both hands. "Go!"

We were on our feet at once, surging toward the door in waves. I was halfway across the room when Bolivar called to me. "Ryuu…"

I stopped, meeting his gaze. "Yeah?"

He grinned. "Not going to use the window?"

Word gets around fast.

Captain Tarique stared coldly, his face only slightly thawed by the ghost of a smile that faded as fast as it came.

I turned away and continued on, Frigg snickering beside me.

~

We'd been at it for hours, breathing through surgical masks, wearing hydrogel-polymer gloves as we searched for unlikely survivors, sifted wreckage for the black box flight recorder, and used tiny flags and transmitters to mark human remains. The burned, chopped up body parts challenged our emotional reserve. Frigg and Gina were with me. We'd all been deployed in teams of three with a backpack of supplies that included an ear-bud comm unit. I had the one for our team and responded as Captain Tarique directed the operation directly.

As more and more professional assistance arrived, they followed in the wake of our teams. It seemed odd not to pull us and let the pros take over. Odder still was the fact that all of us had been issued beamers, not the more common neural stunners. My beamer rode my outer right thigh, strapped down in a holster. I'd found a steel piece of strut that I used as a walking stick; it had the general shape and feel of a kendo sword, just a little heavier.

No edge, but a ragged point. A wanna-be katana.

Still, it felt more natural in my hand than the beamer ever did.

Captain Tarique's voice sounded in my ear. "We weren't sure, there was just a very small chance, so most military units have been tied up at the ports, nailing them down. I can tell you now that recently discovered vid footage confirms an ET presence infiltrating our worlds. On the ARIEL that may have caused the crash. If you find a body that is not quite human, report at once and do not disturb it. Your immunizations protect you from known alien pathogens but let's not take unnecessary chances; mark the site and retreat. A HAZMAT team will take over."

I relayed the message to the girls.

"An alien?" Gena said. "No wonder things have been off. It's why those of us with XT training are clearing the way for official personal. Someone thinks the alien might not be completely dead, or safe."

Frigg smiled. "Lucky us. This could be a historical scavenger hunt. Imagine, prelude to an invasion!"

"Hey," I said. "Here's an intact pair of seats. Bodies, too." I rounded the side to see the corpses better. A woman on the left had been burned badly. Her mouth was still open in a silent scream. Most of her hair had burned away.

Frigg took one look and closed her eyes, swallowing heavily. Her smile stripped away, she took a reflexive step backwards. Gina did the job; activating a radio marker, dropping it on the ground. The body in the right seat had an emergency blanket over it. I pulled it aside with the tip of my walking stick. The blanket had kept her from burning and breathing fire. It hadn't protected her from bruised organs or a broken neck from the fall. Before dying, she'd coughed blood.

I froze a second. There was a hole in her stomach, a big one. A host creature had tried digging its way out of her but hadn't quite managed it. Tendrils connected the creature to the woman's spine. It had been wearing her like an overcoat, making a puppet of her. I bet there were also tendrils to her brain, letting the alien creature tap into her senses. I saw big, black eyes, but no other features.

This gives an all new meaning to being invaded.

Retreating several steps, I gave the necessary orders. "Back away everyone. It's our alien. Beamers out. It's not human; it might still be alive."

Frigg not only retreated but took up a protective position in front of me, drawing her beamer, aiming at the protruding alien. This was procedure; it freed me to focus on comms. I tapped the earbud for transmission. "Cadet Ryuu here. We have a positive alien presence. Be warned, it's a parasite and can hide inside human bodies. We have one. There could be more."

Captain Tarique's voice unfurled in my ear. "A containment team is coming with a cryo-box for transportation of the alien. Take no chances but keep observing. If it's not dead, we don't want it crawling off and hiding."

What he means is—don't let it take a new host.

"Copy," I said.

"Command out."

I tapped the earbud to close the transmission, stepped diagonally forward, and stopped beside the girls. Gina used her beamer muzzle to point at the exposed parasite. "There, poking out from under it, that's a piece of technology I don't recognize."

Frigg spoke without taking her eyes off the potential threat. "I don't think that's human tech, maybe a medical implant or something. The alien looks wired to it. Food supply, transmitter maybe?"

"Transmitter maybe. Not food supply. It seems to have eaten most of the woman's internal organs."

"Eeeeww!" Frigg blanched, but wasn't sick. I was proud of her for not contaminating the scene. We'd have lost points.

"Is the tech still working?" Gina asked.

I shrugged, not seeing any blinking LEDs. "How would I know?"

"You're the one with the weird quantum-field hearing," Gina said.

I held up a hand for silence. I *did* hear something, low, faint, a bit of crystal song in the air. I focused on where it came from. Darting sideways, I moved past Frigg. I still held the strut in my left hand. I slashed it into position in front of me as the quantum inharmonic spiked, a discordant song.

Here is the cause of the crash. Whatever else the aliens intended the device to do, it collapsed the quantum drive on the lunar transport.

The transports with their weaker engines were less heavily shielded, more vulnerable than the star cruisers. This oversight by the aliens had spoiled the landing on Earth, and probably other worlds since the big ships were always launched off-world, planets being serviced by transports.

Our just-discovered enemies had sabotaged themselves from the beginning.

We got so damn lucky.

The alien dissonance faded. I saw movement and responded by reflex. My make-shift sword stabbed into the burned body on the left, the source of the sound I'd heard. A second alien appeared, stabbed through its small body. It writhed, tendrils flailing, y trying to climb the strut to get to me.

Gina fired her beamer. She hit the alien—and the device wired to it. The device popped open, spilling blackened, wire-filled goo. The alien on the strut had stiffened, then relaxed. Maybe dead, maybe not.

"Gina, shoot again if it moves." I looked right. "Frigg, don't shoot again." She'd yelped, startled, and had shot the wrong alien. "We should try not to ruin the specimens more than we have to." I handed the hilt of the strut to Gina. "Here. You watch this one. Frigg will cover the other in case it needs to die again."

Gina took the strut from me. I backed away between them, tapping my earbud. This disrupted the general chatter, giving me an open line to Captain Tarique. I reported. "Cadet Ryuu. Second alien located. All teams are to be cautioned; they *can* survive the crash. One attacked and had to be put down. Keep on your toes."

"Captain Tarique, here. Message received. I'm on my way with the HAZMAT team. Make sure the area is secure. We don't want more surprises."

"Copy," I said.

"Command out."

I tapped my link, shutting down the transmission feature until needed. I was sure we'd be judged on this exercise, including comm discipline, and team work. Unfortunately, Frigg's beaming of a dead target might cost us a point or two. Our personal AIs would have the full experience recorded for download by our teachers.

"You two stay on guard. I've been ordered to secure the perimeter for the incoming team."

"Acknowledged," Gina said.

"Ditto," Frigg said.

I moved off, circling, then spiraling farther out. I looked at everything. Using a bit of branch to turn over loose objects not embedded deeply in the ground. I radio-flagged remains as I found them and kept on. This part of the area had little debris. I finished my sweeps and returned to the girls as a float truck arrived with Captain Tarique and the containment team. The vehicle's quantum field hummed a little unsteadily as it rode a blue glow toward us, stopping a few feet away. The field weakened and the truck settled to the ground.

Frigg stayed on position, weapon on the exposed alien protruding from the corpse. Gina carried the strut with the impaled alien, walking beside me as we went to meet the team. The truck doors opened and a back hatch lifted. That's when I heard the discordant crystal song. It was coming from one of the containment team members. He was containing the alien threat all right. I fired into his abdomen. We had orders. Take no chances.

The man crumpled. The dissonant song ended.

Captain Tarique rushed me and seized my gun hand by the wrist, also gripping my elbow. I stood relaxed, convinced that if I resisted him, he'd break my arm. I allowed him to take my beamer. He stared hard into my face. "What the hell are you doing?" He didn't seem to notice that Gina had her beamer pointed straight at him; a commanding officer is a commander officer, but your team is your life-support.

That will probably cost us a few more points though.

"Captain Tarique, sir. The corpse I shot was a host of these aliens. Cut open the stomach and you'll find one inside, controlling him like a meat puppet."

The Captain stared a moment, then called to the recovery team. "One of you, check it out."

A few minutes later, after a little exploratory surgery, we heard disconcerted gasps. One of the men spoke in a shaky voice. "He's right. An alien presence."

Captain Tarique released me and barked orders. "Get the aliens packed away. The human corpses go too. I want all cadets to stay with me for debriefing." The HAZMAT team did their job. The Captain interrupted them just once to study the box from the alien Frigg guarded. He said, "Make sure the alien tech gets to our techs at R&D for study." The girls joined me when relieved of their aliens. They stood beside me, relaxed, not quite parade rest. We weren't yet enlisted; we didn't need to honor military protocol, just be respectful.

As the truck readied for departure, Captain Tarique came back to me. "Cadet Ryuu, your weapon." He handed me back my beamer. "How did you know we had a ringer in our midst?"

"Unique personal ability, Sir. Those boxes of theirs put out an inharmonic tone that interferes with quantum fields. I…heard it."

"I didn't." Captain Tarique shifted his stare to Frigg and Gina. "You two hear anything?"

They answered in unison. "No, Sir!"

The Captain's gaze came back to me. This time, he had more than the ghost of a smile on his face. "Son, you have just been conscripted into the X-Corps Intelligence Service. Congratulations. You're our new secret weapon."

THE DIGGINS

Amy Rogers

*A*CCESS RESTRICTED.

Dr. Jeremiah Mallory slid a finger over the wall map in the visitor center. He'd hoped that maybe his information was wrong. But the drive up from the Bay Area hadn't changed the facts. Part of the Diggins was officially off limits. If he went prospecting there, he'd have to do it without permission, like a claim jumper from olden times.

I ought to have some rights, he thought peevishly. *This mine would've failed without my family's involvement.*

Sighing, he bought a waterproof topographic map, a pack of Twinkies and some extra bug spray at the gift shop. Good thing he had packed long pants despite the August heat. He would have to bushwhack to reach the site from the back side of the park, and poison oak was in season.

Why did it have to be so difficult?

Taking a bite of Twinkie he reflected that it could be worse. Back in the 1800s when his great-great-grandfather Hamilton Smith engineered the Malakoff Mine tunnel eight thousand feet through solid bedrock, a guy like Jeremiah—a microbiology professor with soft hands and a weak back—would've been crushed like mine tailings. His quest for modern-day riches required more brains than brawn. Still, as he sat in the front seat of his hybrid SUV and studied the map of Malakoff Diggins State Park and its environs, he knew he was in for some physical exertion.

After he exited Highway 49, the road twisted and narrowed. Oaks and maples yielded to pines and fir trees in the gradually thinning air. 2500 feet higher than where he'd started, he opened the windows to the warm mountain air and the fragrance of sap. He paused on a bridge over Humbug Creek and hung his head out like an eager dog. Sparkling water tinkled over smooth rocks downstream from the old gold mines. A scrub jay called from the trees.

Jeremiah looked at the gear bag in his backseat. He hadn't crossed the park boundary yet. He had permission from the landowner here to sample the water. The guy had been thrilled to sign the legal papers. If Jeremiah found what he was looking for, and successfully manipulated it in his laboratory, the other man would get a small cut of the profits. A small piece of what was potentially a very large pie.

Might as well try.

He parked on the shoulder of the road and extracted a sampling kit from his bag. Over the past six months he'd measured the amount of mercury in creeks and rivers across a hundred miles of the Sierra Nevada foothills. To some extent, mercury was everywhere, a toxic legacy of the Gold Rush. He knew this creek was contaminated. Any microorganisms in the water would necessarily have adapted to survive in the presence of the heavy metal. Maybe he would find his mercury-tolerant bacteria here.

He leaned over the bank and deftly plunged a small apparatus into the frigid, clear water. Thank God he didn't have to stand in an icy stream, bent over, panning for gold all day long. As his fingers turned white with cold he pumped water across a microbiologic filter to trap invisible life forms. Later in his laboratory, he would study their DNA in search of a superpower—the ability to decontaminate methyl mercury. If he could design an artificial microbe to clean up mercury contamination, the patent would be worth millions for bioremediation.

Millions.

Though he labeled and stowed the filter, he'd made up his mind. The most powerful mutations would be found in bacteria surviving in the highest concentration of mercury. Sure, this creek had some mercury in it. But not enough, not for his purpose.

He needed to follow the poison.

The SUV, long accustomed to urban pavement, eagerly chewed up the gravel road. Jeremiah noted the odometer reading and counted the miles and tenths as he skirted the state park. Braking, he consulted the map one more time. Yes, from here was the shortest line to the territory he wanted to sample. No trails, and through a crosshatched area on the map. Restricted access. He tried to discern if the area was private or public land, but the map's legend was unclear. Whatever. If he found what he was looking for, who could say the specimen didn't come from Humbug Creek?

What mattered was finding the bacteria, and this forbidden location was his best hope. His mercury data indicated that the streams flowing from this area were the most contaminated in the region. They came from a part of the Diggins active in the mine's heyday in the 1870s, when the North Bloomfield Mining and Gravel Company blasted the mountains into rubble with high-pressure water cannons in a heedlessly destructive extraction process called hydraulic mining. Tens of thousands of tons of gravel every day washed into huge sluices where the gold was trapped and mixed with elemental mercury. Mercury reacted with gold, forming a dense amalgam that captured even the smallest gold flakes. In the process, mercury escaped into the environment. By the time the Gold Rush ended, millions of pounds of mercury were left behind.

There's a cache of mercury somewhere up there, he thought. *It's leaching into the streams. The closer I get, the higher the concentration will be.*

He had no worries for his health. Methyl mercury couldn't hurt him as long as he didn't drink the water. Elemental mercury only poisoned humans if it was vaporized and inhaled—and then it drove them mad.

He loaded a backpack with his scientific equipment and simple camping gear for one night under the stars. The hike to the mine was about five miles. Forging his way through underbrush would be slow. He planned to spend the night near the source, do a thorough sampling in the morning, and return to his car tomorrow. The forecast predicted a warm, dry night. No need to carry a tent. A light sleeping bag and mosquito netting on poles would be enough shelter.

Choosing a slight break in the vegetation along the road, he plunged in. After a mere three or four strides he came to a sign, pocked with holes from shotgun pellets.

NO TRESPASSING.

Definitely not building a fire tonight. Got to keep a low profile.

Settling the weight of his pack on his hips, he pressed on. Woody shrubs and young conifers choked the forest floor. Everywhere he looked he counted leaves of three: poison oak as tall as his knees, and higher. Damn.

The shadiest areas had less undergrowth. He gravitated toward them, brushing cobwebs from his face. A crust of sticky burrs grew on his boots. After an hour following his compass, he stopped to take a piss under a particularly dark canopy of trees where the air was hot and still with an odor of decay. As he watered the ground, the stream of his urine washed aside some of the pine needles and leafy matter.

Something appeared underneath.

A flat stone of some kind was buried here, brownish-red like a brick. With the sole of his boot he scraped away more of the plant debris. His foot snagged on rough-edged depressions in the stone. It was writing, carved into the rock.

He zipped his pants and squatted for a closer look. The marks were Asian characters of some kind. Old. Forgotten. Chinese?

For a moment he froze, recalling a family ghost story. His cousins would tell it when his mother wasn't there to hush them, a story about the Chinese laborers who dug Hamilton Smith's famous tunnel. His father let the older boys tell it once, and as they embellished the miners' deaths with imaginative, gruesome detail, his father said it was a good thing they didn't have tort lawyers in those days.

Jeremiah swept the earth with his feet. Was he standing at the site of a 19th century Chinese mining camp? He uncovered a brass button and a small glass bottle, smashed with the shards held together by a paper label written in Chinese.

Interesting, but not on his agenda today. He checked the time and his direction. A mournful breeze unexpectedly gusted through, stirring some leaves and exposing a broken fragment of terra cotta. He paused. *Very* interesting. He felt an intense desire to examine it. What was the rush anyway? Dropping to his knees, he turned the fragment over in his hands. What did it break off from? He plunged his fingers into the dirt, and dug. The soil resisted. He pushed harder, curling his thumbs, disturbing all manner of crawling things that slithered away from his assault. He uncovered more terra cotta, the rest of a disk, a lid or cover of some kind.

The curiosity was irresistible. He scrambled to find a stick to pry the lid up. A jar was buried here.

What was inside? He had to know, but it was dark in the hole.

Flashlight!

A centipede slithered out of the jar, away from the light. He angled the beam to reach deeper.

Inside, a jumble of—*bones.*

The raucous call of a crow broke his reverie. He blinked and looked at his filthy hands. Worse than dirt, a poison oak plant lay uprooted nearby. Did he pull that up? What had he been thinking? Had he just opened a *grave*?

Ashamed, he slid the broken lid back onto the burial jar and covered it with leaves. Then he wiped his hands on his pants as best he could—probably futile, if poison oak oil was on them—and implored himself to remember not to touch his face. As he briskly strode away from the lost Chinese camp, his stomach churned. That jar. Remains of an animal, right? A pony? Some kind of traditional Chinese medicine product?

Twenty minutes later he came to a stream where he rinsed his hands over and over. Without soap to wash away the oil, he was probably going to break out in a painful, itchy rash. It would be hours or days until he knew for sure. He bent over the water again, reaching—

His weight shifted suddenly.

The stream was less than a foot deep, but it certainly was wet, and cold. He shouted curses and clambered to his feet, ready to confront whoever had pushed him in.

Of course he was alone in the wilderness. Just slippery rocks and lousy balance. He wrung his socks. This hike was turning out to be a crappy idea. But the potential payday from a discovery…

With the stream as a guide, he no longer had to navigate. The terrain was rough and his shoes were wet. He day-dreamed about money until the sun sank low in the sky and he finally reached the manmade cliff of the Diggins, an ugly, barren remnant of the hydraulic mine. Rubble covered the area around the cliff and buried the source of the stream he'd followed. Tomorrow he would collect microbial specimens here and anywhere he could find water. For now, rest.

The rubble pile seemed an inhospitable place for a sleeping bag, but as he turned to find a better campsite, a wave of exhaustion swept over him. One step away from the cliff, and his eyelids drooped. Two steps, and he nearly fainted. He staggered back to the wall and luckily noticed a sandy area at the base of the cliff. Smooth and oddly clear of rocks, the spot was just big enough for him to stretch out. The funky smell he noticed in the air wouldn't keep him awake. He wolfed down a sandwich, then collapsed into sleep.

Itching haunted his dreams. He dreamt of blisters, raised and red, covering the skin of his hands and forearms. His dream-hands scratched and scratched to no avail.

At first light he woke, his mouth dry and his bedding damp with condensation. His feet itched and he writhed inside his sleeping bag, rubbing his soles against each other. The narrow mummy bag strangled him. He tore at the zipper and freed himself.

No sign of poison oak rash on his hands (yet), but so many mosquito bites on his ankles and heels! Why else would his skin itch so badly? Munching on a granola bar, he danced back and forth in his sandals, constantly bending over to scratch. The sun rose higher and illuminated the cliff. In a knife of bright sunbeam, he noticed a faint silvery mist emanating from the rock. A cave. Last night in the dim light and bowed by his weirdly urgent fatigue, he hadn't noticed the opening. It was rectangular and narrow but tall enough to walk through. Not a cave, he corrected himself. A tunnel, with water trickling out.

His heart pounded faster. Surely this was an old mining tunnel, perhaps even the tunnel Hamilton Smith built. Could it be the source of the excessive mercury contamination in this area? Quickly he performed a spot test of the water. The mercury level was off the charts. *I was right to come here*, he rejoiced. The prospects for his bioprospecting looked better than ever. Even though he didn't have proper gear for spelunking, he could get samples from a little ways inside. He had to do it. Now.

Quickly he donned shoes, a sweatshirt and his backpack of sampling equipment and hurried to the entrance of the mountain. Turning sideways, he slipped into the maw, where he noticed writing on the rock. Jagged letters were scrawled around the opening. Wait—not letters. They were Chinese characters, dark on the pale rock. He touched the damp stone. To his surprise, his fingers smeared the marks. Black smudges obscured the strokes and blackened moisture dripped down the wall. Something like charcoal soiled his hands. He rubbed them together and the itching flared in his legs. If the writing dissolved in water, how did it survive a hundred years?

He vowed to get in there, get the samples, and go home.

As the mountain swallowed him, he turned on his small handheld flashlight. In a few steps, cool damp air chilled his bones. He shivered, once, a subtle tremor that started in his toes, glided to his shoulders and ended in his tingling fingers. A metallic taste filled his mouth. A few steps farther down the tunnel, the light from the entrance diminished shockingly fast. He hesitated, and thick silence smothered him. The only sound was the dripping of water and...

Is that a voice? Is someone else down here?

He shook his head. Overactive imagination.

He strode swiftly, recklessly, in a bubble of light that briefly displaced the heavy blackness as if he were piloting a bathysphere through an ocean of ink. The bacteria he was looking for could be anywhere. He came upon a puddle and collected a few milliliters of water from it. He grinned. Bacteria in that water would have genes allowing them to tolerate mercury. Had he struck gold?

Not yet, the voice said, more clearly this time.

After pausing a full minute to scratch his ankles, he labeled and stashed the water sample and continued deeper into the mountain, collecting as he went. Something was in the air, the strange odor he'd noticed at his campsite now become a reek. The mercury level in the water was so high it exceeded the range of his test kit. Tremors shook his body. This was his mother lode.

On slick ground he staggered farther and farther down the tunnel. The air grew warmer, and for the first time the passage branched. An old wood door and a DANGER sign blocked access to the other tunnel.

Is that light? Gingerly he approached the door and turned off his flashlight. A faint glow seemed to outline the door, but if he looked at it directly, it disappeared. He touched the door, letting his fingers trace some of the many initials carved into the wood. It felt warm, definitely warmer than the surrounding rock. Hesitantly he lifted the padlock and rusted chain.

No way in.

Shaking his head, he kept going. How far was far enough? *Deeper.* The voice told him he had to go deeper. He stumbled and stubbed his toe and automatically reached down to rub it. Yet there was no pain, and no itching either. In fact, he could barely feel his feet anymore. Dizzy, he braced himself against the narrowing walls.

Look. You found it.

The beam from his flashlight reflected off something on the floor of the tunnel: a shiny pebble. He sagged to his knees and picked it up. Gold? It couldn't be. Could it? He pocketed the pebble. Suddenly genetic engineering seemed like a lot of unnecessary effort. Wobbling in place, he searched the area for more golden reflections. A tiny fleck in the wall. He scratched at it with his fingers. Gold!

If his progress before had been slow, it now became a crawl, sometimes literally as he moved on hands and knees, hunting for gold. *Lab work is dumb. This is easier.* The flecks and fragments were few but his pocket stash grew. He laughed maniacally. *My tunnel. My gold.*

At some point he noticed the knees of his pants were torn and bloody. He sat back heavily against the wall. Why was his backpack missing? Tilting his head to stretch his neck, he scanned the vicinity for gleams. Above him, something glittered. Not golden. Silvery.

He struggled to stand and peered closely at the ceiling of the tunnel for the first time. It was coated with tiny crystals, beautiful, symmetric, that shattered the light into a thousand fragments. He extended a finger to touch the crystals. The finger twitched uncontrollably, and he stabbed himself on a crystalline spike. A drop of blood formed and fell to the ground, followed by another droplet from the crystal. This liquid was neither red nor watery, but silver.

Muttering under his breath, he stared at the fallen bead of mercury as it glistened in the light of his lamp. It rolled and shifted, then stretched out like a snake. Unblinking he watched as the liquid metal formed itself into a pattern, lines bending and crossing. For a moment he thought he saw it create a tiny Chinese character. Then the quicksilver gradually vanished.

The itching in his feet flared intense, unbearable. He ripped off his shoes and scratched without relief. He scratched harder. Harder. It wasn't enough. He groped the floor for a sliver of stone and scratched it across his soles. Harder. Pain and itching blurred together. The stone broke the skin.

Then he felt the crawling things.

With one hand he tried to brush them away, while the other hand wielded the flashlight, trying to spot them, scare them away. But they were invisible. Swatting frantically, he dropped the light. Bugs crawled over his bare feet and burrowed under his skin, silent, numerous, relentless. He tried to stamp them out. They started to climb up his legs. He scratched and rubbed to sweep them away. They invaded his hands. He shouted obscenities into the darkness. They were multiplying. On the move. Unseen insects under his skin, wriggling.

A voice cried, *This way! This way!*

A pale glow and warm air beckoned. He staggered forward, flailing his arms. A hot breeze touched his face.

The bugs climbed up to his elbows and knees. Distant voices called him. *Hamilton! We have your riches!*

But my name is—

Insects crawled up his neck, squirmed under his scalp. He staggered, screaming, and tore at his hair.

The door was open. A rusted chain and a DANGER sign lay on the floor like a tile. His torn, bare foot left a bloody print.

Come for your treasure, Hamilton Smith! they cried.

He ran toward the glow, around a corner. A shimmer on the wall. Bugs and bugs and bugs—

A silver pool on the ground, bubbling gently. For a moment he hesitated, something deep in his brain warning him to stop. He stepped one foot into the glittering pool. The liquid was heavy, hot. It soothed the itching. Yes! Eagerly he immersed the other foot.

The insects under his skin quieted. Any hesitation left him. He had to be rid of them. He knelt, parting the quicksilver that beaded and rolled over his thighs. Relief flowed into the submerged parts of his body. He lowered his arms into the pool but his scalp still seethed. He lay back. The remaining bugs fled the cleansing liquid and crowded onto his face. He screamed. They filled his open mouth.

The voices spoke a strange, singsong language. He sank beneath the surface and heard no more.

DELBERT'S TREE

Dennis Grayson

The silly behavior of the squirrels first drew young Delbert Pelfrey's attention to the imposing, old oak tree shielding the ground beneath its drip line. Rising dead center in the town square park, it towered protectively above the maples, buckeyes, and other trees scattered to the four corners of the commons. Other than its near perfect placement and size, the only other oddity the oak presented was a perfectly circular eight-inch knothole positioned exactly five feet above the lawn. And, of course, there were the screwy squirrels.

Today, Delbert sat on weathered wood slats supported by a well-patinated wrought iron frame bench, just where he had when he visited the town square for over fifty-five years. Facing the oak, he could keep tabs on the bushy-tailed critters. He had brought a paper grocery sack with him and plopped it beside him on the bench. He made a quick scan of the area to see if the squirrels paid any attention to him. Nope. The plump, grey creatures totally ignored him.

Well, he thought, it is the winter side of autumn. These guys are hoarding nuts for the wave of blizzards soon to rush down on central Ohio from the Great Lakes. Memories of the knife-like gusts of frigid, Arctic air sent a shiver through him. Then he bit his lip and shrugged. "Doesn't matter," he mumbled. "I won't make it to Thanksgiving Day."

Crumpling the edge of the bag, he looked around once more to see if he could distract the squirrels. No luck again. They remained diligent in their tasks. Most of them carried acorns in their mouths. Dozens of the critters, lugging their loads effortlessly, scurried to the tree, scampered up the trunk, and deposited their booty by dumping it inside the knothole. Then they hurried away for another future meal.

"Chick-chick!"

He raised his field of vision to a branch higher in the tree where he found Bucky, the boss squirrel, admonishing him for trying to disrupt the day's work plan.

"Chick-chick!"

Delbert smiled and shook his head. "Take it easy!" he yelled up at the squirrel. "A little paper rattling isn't the worst you're going to face in the coming days!" He pulled the morning newspaper out of the bag, unfolded it, and showed the front page to Bucky. "See this?"

"Chick!" Bucky turned his head sideways, as if trying to read the headline.

"Sez here that the state parks people are coming to study this tree of yours. They figure it's well over two hundred years old—that the town square was built around it. This is a picture of your tree taken in 1858, when the town was only fifty years old. Your acorn hiding place looks exactly the same as it does now. They want to know why. There's gonna be a small army of white-coats pruning, boring, and scrapping at the tree. What do you think about that?"

Bucky's tail bristled and flicked several times. "Chick!"

"Yeah, that's my thinking also," said Delbert, as he reached back into the sack and pulled out a sandwich encased in a plastic baggie—bologna and white bread with a generous helping of real mayo.

The taste of his first bite of the sandwich took him right back to early childhood. Many a time he had sat on this very bench savoring pimento loaf, cotto salami, olive loaf, or bologna lunches while following the antics of Bucky and his pals. Back in the 1950s, the square was a thriving commerce center. Department stores, a five-and-dime store, record shops, two theaters, the county courthouse and jail, hole-in-the-wall eateries, and a dozen other assorted small businesses ringed the park. None of the buildings topped out at over five stories high. Autos ranging from older Model A pickups to the newest chrome-embellished, two-toned sedans circled counter-clockwise, continually searching out a convenient parking space. Three graying monuments marked the sacrifices of young men and women lost in The Civil War, The War to End All Wars, and The Second World War. Despite the drifting clouds of vehicle exhaust fumes, the air in the park held a woodsy fragrance.

A lot of the square had changed over the decades. The department stores now sat vacant, slowly filling with ever rising sediment of dust, pigeon guano, and worse. Only one theater remained in operation, specializing in triple-X features. Few cars parked downtown anymore, so spaces sat empty, displaying iridescent, multicolored oil splotches. For the hungry, their choices were down to a franchise torpedo sandwich shop and the barely surviving George's Coney Island Hot Dogs. Four-lettered graffiti disgraced the monuments to fallen heroes. The vegetation in the park was either unpruned and overgrown, or dried out and withering. Only the central oak remained vibrant.

Why is that? Delbert pondered. The tree received no more water or nutrients than the others. He chuckled to himself. Maybe squirrel pee fed and watered the tree—there were enough of them to do the job—dozens and dozens of them. It had to be the squirrels; no other animals were allowed to approach the oak. Bucky and his bushy-tailed gang ran off all other critters, even dogs twenty-five times their size. His face contorted with disgust as he flashed back to a chilling memory of the squirrels taking down and killing a full-grown black Labrador retriever which had urinated on the tree trunk.

That was back in 1954, just months after Delbert noticed the change in Bucky.

Actually, Delbert noticed the weird sound coming out of the knot-hole first. Then a week or so later, Bucky went hostile. Up until the change, Bucky greedily grabbed peanuts and other treats out of Delbert's hand and sat calmly and cutely eating them while only inches away from Delbert's feet. Thereafter, the boss squirrel chattered angrily at Delbert if he came any closer than a few yards to the oak or any of the gang. One time Bucky had actually charged him and nipped viciously at his shoe. Luckily, he had worn Oxfords that day instead of his usual canvas Keds.

It was hard to describe the oak tree's sound. As a kid, Delbert had never visited the ocean, but he had held a buddy's sea shell up to his ear to listen to the roar of white noise. Larry Nelson told him that was what breakers on the beach sounded like—and he was an authority because he and his family traveled all the way to Myrtle Beach, South Carolina every summer. The knot-hole sound was similar, but off just a bit—not soothing, but irritating. Images of an ocean did not fill Delbert's mind, instead he envisioned far off, sinister space realms—places of darkness and deformed clusters of energy clouds.

The knot-hole scared Delbert. One encounter put him off ever trying to look into the cavity again. He did not want to know what caused the sound.

On the other hand, the knot-hole seemed to fascinate the squirrels. Even so, it had taken several days for them to edge closer and closer.

Bucky was the first to poke his head past the threshold and drop into the hollow. When he emerged, moments later, Bucky was a changed animal. He was The Boss—his pelt silkier—his eyes brighter—his demeanor no longer timid. Standing erect on the lower lip of the hole, he split the air with a mighty high-pitched peal that was surely heard blocks away over the bustling town center background noise. Bushy-tails from all over the park scrambled down tree trunks and assembled at the base of the oak resting on their haunches. Looking like the mayor at a town meeting, Bucky nattered at the assemblage. Young Delbert had no idea what Bucky said, but the gathered squirrels listened attentively—a few scratched at their ears with their hind feet, but they paid attention. Then, in clusters of five or six, all the critters took turns entering the tree cavity. Upon exiting, these little animals also had a more intelligent look about them. Falling into a rough platoon-like formation, the furry creatures waited patiently as Bucky finished his "speech."

With a delighted child's giggle, Delbert distracted the proceedings. Squirrel heads turned toward him. Black, button eyes glared a warning. Delbert felt unsettled—intimidated. What had happened to his wee pals? He ran home that afternoon, and at bedtime hid under his sheet and blanket, all the time not wanting to believe what he had seen. That was why he went back to the park each day after school. He was impelled to confirm his suspicions, even if those suspicions scared the bejesus out of him.

Within days, Bucky ordered…no…commanded the gang through complicated work processes. He assigned several squirrels to lookout detail. From high in the oak, two kept watch on the square, screeching out warnings if any dogs or cats entered the grounds. Other squirrels took up positions on the courthouse roof. From there they could see an approaching storm or other danger. Most of the gang gathered nuts, pounds and pounds of nuts, and deposited them in the oak tree's hollow. Others were sent out on foraging sorties. They came back from all directions hauling cheeks full of pretzels, chips, discarded pizza crusts, and a myriad of stale edibles. These were all added to their hoard, which Bucky, like a greedy corporate financial officer, kept tabs on throughout the day from his perch on the lip of the knot-hole. Withdrawals were only allowed late in the evening with Bucky deciding how much food each worker would get.

Young Delbert, not mature enough to understand government in action, sensed none of the behavior was normal. He tried to tell Dad about it once, but his father dismissed him with a snicker and told him to get ready for bed.

Squirrel behavior took a darker twist when the foragers first hauled back hotdog hunks. These were not saved in the tree hole, but were voraciously devoured at sunset each day. Delbert looked up "squirrels" in the family Encyclopedia Britannica. They were described as being herbivores. Further research on that word led him to the antonym, carnivores—flesh eaters. Bucky and the gang had become omnivores. He looked that word up also.

Yep, that screwed up my naïve child mind for a few months, thought senior citizen Delbert. I had my own private B-horror tale playing out right in front of me every day.

He began to drop the half-eaten bologna sandwich back into the baggie, then thought of a better idea. Ever since the second round of chemotherapy, all food tasted off to him. He ate enough to keep going, but enjoyed none of it. It seemed a waste to let perfectly good bologna spoil, so he slipped the remainder of two slices out from between the bread. "You guys want this?" he called out to the squirrels.

Bucky looked at him and bopped in place. "Chicka-chicka-chicka-chick!"

"I'm guessin' that's a yes." He gave the partial disks of meat an underhanded, Frisbee fling. They splatted into the tree trunk and flopped to the ground.

"Annnk!" That order from Bucky sent three of his gang scuttling across the lawn to take up a protective perimeter around the booty. The squirrels were as organized as ever.

Delbert thought back to 1973, the year he returned from Vietnam after serving as an Army 21B2 combat engineer. Barely adjusted to wearing civvies again, he revisited the haunt of his childhood, the town square. Sitting on the familiar bench he discovered that in the three years he'd been in the military the behavior of the squirrels had warped to an even more malevolent level. Not satisfied with warning off only other animals, Bucky turned the squirrels' wrath toward humans. They chased after children and adults, chattering and barking while threatening to nip at human ankles. Few people now entered the park, and those that did were mostly maintenance workers armed with mowers, rakes and shovels. For some unknown reason Bucky allowed Delbert to continue to visit. Within weeks, the downtown business operators were calling the oak "Delbert's Tree." The squirrels were dubbed a nuisance and referred to as "those damn rodents!"

A sort of war broke out. Junior high kids, armed with BB guns, stalked the square on Friday nights taking potshots at the vermin. The police knew about this activity, but never seemed to have a squad car in the vicinity when the juveniles were on the prowl. Bucky's crew gave as good as they got. They would lay in wait on tree branches, dropping on heads and biting and scratching scalps and ears. Several adolescent hunters ended a night with scabby nicks and sutures.

When Animal Control came to investigate the attacks, they could never find a single squirrel. Stomping around the park for an hour or more netted nothing. Bucky's gang simply vanished. And Delbert knew where they had gone—the knot-hole. Well, most of them anyway. A couple hid under the Animal Control vehicle waiting for the two "dogcatchers" to wander to the far side of the park, then the squirrels unscrewed the valve-stem caps and let the air out of the truck's tires. Delbert found this funny and disturbing.

Soon the little devils expanded their vandalism to other vehicles parked around the square. Every few days a shopper would return to his or her car or truck to find at least one flat tire. People quickly learned to park in lots away from the town center.

This contributed to the slow decay of the area. Who wanted to walk halfway across downtown to buy an LP or a pair of flared jeans? Other factors were the closing of three major manufacturing plants located just a dozen blocks north of the square, the opening of sprawling discount stores out in the county, and the youth movement from "this hick town" to larger, hipper urban Meccas.

This also meant no job opportunities in town for a freshly discharged veteran. Fortunately, Delbert's training as a combat engineer qualified him for a starting position with the Ohio Department of Transportation. He transitioned from neutralizing booby traps and placing mines to boring holes and placing charges for highway construction. The work paid well, but kept him out of town at least five days a week. Visits with Bucky and the gang were cut down to a few days a month for over a decade. Then work began on sections and ramps on I-71 nearer to town. He got to go home to his apartment every night and hang out at the town square more often.

One Saturday night, after a calzone and a pitcher of beer at Esposito's, Delbert slumped on the bench, his mind drifted to concerns he had shoved aside for a long time. This was 1988, almost thirty-five years since the altered Bucky had emerged from the knot-hole. Could that really be? Was Bucky over three decades old? Did squirrels live that long? Were all the critters that old? A bunch of them had identifying marks and they were still around. And what about that knothole? How many nuts would it hold? The squirrels must have tossed tons of nuts and junk in there. How did the tree hold it all? Maybe it didn't hold it. Maybe it sent it someplace. Where?

Delbert did something he had not tried for a very long time. He approached the oak. Weaving a bit, he shook his head to clear his beer-buzz.

"Chick! Chick!"

Bucky spotted him.

"Easy, buddy. Just gonna take me a little look-see."

Scrambling down the trunk, Bucky vehemently chastised the interloper.

Delbert put out his hands to brace himself on the oak as he turned his head to listen with his right ear. Yep, the roaring sound was as loud and irritating as he remembered.

The squirrel boss nipped at his fingers. Delbert shrugged off the annoyance. "Forget it, Bucky. You're not chasing me off this time. I'm going to see just what's going on in that hole."

"Chicka-chick!" Bucky scratched at Delbert's hand, opening oozing wounds.

"Ouch! Dammit! Knock it off!" He flicked the squirrel aside with a brush of his hand.

Leaning forward, Delbert's head penetrated the opening. Now the ocean-like sound came at him from all directions, swirling about and flowing downward, as if he were in a large drainpipe. But there was no air resistance. The effect was dizzying. His eyes, tracking the movement of the sound, glanced down. The cavity was empty, not a nut or pizza crust to be found. What the…? Where did all the stuff go?

Tiny, clawed feet scampered up his neck and over his skull, coming to a stop just above his forehead.

"Ennnnk!"

So close that his eyes crossed, Bucky's face hung upside down in Delbert's field of vision. One paw arced downward and took a warning swipe at his eyes. Delbert pushed back on the tree trunk with all of his strength and fell to the ground with a thump. Bucky rolled off his head and tumbled another six feet before stopping.

Delbert lay there for the longest time fearing to move. He sensed something in him had altered permanently. His beer-buzz was gone, replaced by a more natural and harmonious tingle of contented bliss. His senses were sharper. Individual blades of grass pressing into his back could be counted through layers of clothing. Incense fragrance from the Catholic church five blocks distant tickled his nose as if burning beside him. Straight up, stars drifted closer, until he felt sure he could reach out and grasp one. Inside his head, the roaring noise from the oak tree continued to reverberate. With it came the compulsions to take, control, and suppress—feelings Delbert never before experienced. These grated at that part of him he thought of as his soul, as if attempting to shave away layers of ingrained moral and ethical values. This terrified him more than the first time he had to disarm a live Claymore mine.

He felt squirrel feet walking on him again. This time they climbed onto his chest and timidly approached his face.

"Chick?"

"Yeah. I'm okay, buddy." Delbert gingerly rose to a sitting position with Bucky hanging onto his shirt with all four paws. "I don't know what you see when you go into that knot hole, but it damn well isn't anything I want to see ever again."

"Chick-chick."

"No, it's not good. It's evil."

"Chick!"

"Well, you can keep it all to yourself."

Satisfied, Bucky leaped off Delbert and scampered back to the oak.

That was the last time Delbert ever approached the tree. He contented himself with keeping tabs on the squirrels from a distance.

Now, twenty years later, the back of Delbert's hand still exhibited the scars from that day. There was also a smattering of age spots. Permanent yellow stains made his fingernails look sickly and cadaverous. One knuckle swollen by arthritis refused to bend. His hand, like the rest of his body, was succumbing to time and disease. Liver cancer, triggered by decades of handling RDX explosives, was near to claiming a final victory—perhaps only weeks away. And that was why he had to take action now.

He called out. "Bucky!"

The squirrel's head pivoted to look him in the eye. "Chick?"

Delbert rose to his feet and stood next to the bench.

Bucky now poised on the lip of the knot-hole, bristled, as if expecting danger.

"I don't know how much of this you can understand, Bucky, but you squirrels are not normal. This tree is not normal. It's changed you into a little dictator. The others have become too smart…too mean." Delbert reached into the grocery sack and took out the newspaper. "You are all over sixty years old. I don't know how the tree did it, but we…I can't let the scientists find out. And they will find out when they come to inspect the tree." He waved the newspaper to make his point.

Bucky cocked his head side to side as if trying to comprehend what Delbert was saying. "Chick?"

"The point is, it's no longer going to be just you squirrels with…ah…enhanced minds. It'll be dangerous…catastrophic if humans are enhanced."

"Chick!" Bucky's mouth opened wide, as if to snarl, his teeth seemed longer and sharper.

Delbert tossed the paper into a nearby trash can. "My point exactly. Look how angry and aggressive you are. Remember, I know what it's like. My head has been inside that knot- hole.

I still get those feelings. It's not me. I don't like it." He picked up the grocery bag.

"Innnk!" A warning went out to the gang.

With a tentative step toward the tree, Delbert said, "Imagine what the military will do with the tree, Bucky. They'll take it away from you." He took another step.

"Chick!"

"They will, buddy. They'll take it and make something perverted with it—leaders and soldiers with tons of aggression and no conscience to hold them in check." Moving closer, he pulled a brick of Cyclonite, commercial RDX, out of the bag. It was a tree-clearing explosive with an expired "use by" date. Older explosives were to be returned to the manufacturer. This brick wouldn't make it back. The miscount would be noticed in a few days and would be immediately reported to the Feds. It wouldn't matter by then.

Squirrels, by the dozens, gathered in the oak and on the ground as Bucky's distressed bark evolved into a shrill keen.

Reaching into the bag again, Delbert fished out a partial roll of duct tape and an electric blasting cap with a priming adaptor and two wire loops attached. "It's no use carrying on like that, Bucky. As they say, the jig is up." He inserted the cap into the predrilled hole in one end of the Cyclonite block. Taking one last step toward the tree, he secured the wires to the explosive with the duct tape. He stood at the base of the oak and glanced around.

Now, all the squirrels barked, hissed, and chattered insanely. Delbert felt sure they would swarm over him, tearing away his flesh. He hurried his next action, lifting a

12-volt rectangular battery out of the bag, nearly dropping it. The grocery sack did slip away and fall to the ground. Before it could blow away, he knelt and anchored it with the battery.

One squirrel took advantage of the distraction to leap onto Delbert's back. He felt the sharp sting of two incisors cutting at his right shoulder blade. Cradling the explosive with his left arm, he picked the squirrel off with his right, and tossed the bushy-tail into the knot-hole, barely missing Bucky. There was a sound like a lemon seed being sucked into and up a straw. Delbert had no idea if that was good news or bad news for the Kamikaze squirrel. It didn't really matter.

"Sorry."

"Chick!" Bucky stood on his hind legs, scrabbling wildly at Delbert with his front paws.

"I said I was sorry!" He settled onto his butt, resting his back against the tree trunk. Looking up, back over his shoulder, he added, "It's not too late for you all to make a run for it."

Bucky settled onto four paws and studied Delbert for a moment. "Chick?"

"Sure. That is if you want to. Right now, you better move aside."

Hanging upside down on the bark, Bucky moved to a spot a foot below the opening to the hollow.

Delbert reached up and chucked the Cyclonite block into the hole. Holding onto the end of the dual wires, he played out the rest until he was sure the explosive was dangling below the ground line. He called out, "Last chance!"

Bucky screamed, "Annnk!"

All the squirrels in the town square went silent. The moment extended for several seconds, before Bucky crept lower down the tree. Delbert wasn't sure what the squirrel boss was up too. Another attack? Gnaw the wires?

Retrieving the battery, Delbert wedged it between his inner thighs. He felt Bucky's little feet pick their way across his shoulder. Then, a nuzzle of soft fur caressed his chin. He readied the stripped wire tips to make contact. There was no bite to his throat. Instead, the feet moved down the front of his shirt. A fluffy tail twitched at him.

"What are you up to, Bucky?"

The squirrel made it to Delbert's lap.

Oh, Lord, don't let him bite me there.

Bucky circled four times, kneading at Delbert's trouser fabric. Then he settled in, curled into a ball, and looked up at Delbert. "Chick."

"Yeah I'll miss you too." He gently stroked Bucky's head. "We're going to save the world from itself, and no one will ever know about it."

Delbert touched the wires to the battery terminals.

PORKERGEISTS

Judy Prey

L ARRY BOUGHT THE FARM sight unseen. The old owner was in a hurry to sell it, livestock and crops included. The old fart said the pigs might be a big problem, though. The new owner didn't care. The place was cheap and a quick drive out of L.A. *Buying the farm means you were dead, doesn't it?* Too many of his former pals would be happy to dig the hole for him. If they found him and their money, that is.

What to do first? He lied when he said he lived on a farm as a kid. He didn't know shit about animals or growing stuff and didn't care.

After stowing his new stolen car in the garage, Larry looked down the long lane in front of the brown clapboard house. *No trace of a tail. Good so far.*

The place smelled as bad as his old neighborhood. He went inside the house, to the kitchen in the back. He dropped his meager belongings on the worn table. He took a deep breath of relief and gagged. The smell of pig wafted through the open window. A gentle breeze ruffled the lacy curtains.

Pig meant bacon. He liked bacon. He could take a pig to a butcher. On second thought, he couldn't take the risk of someone knowing where he lived. He reached into his duffle and pulled out his .38. Checking the cylinder, he walked out the back door. *Got to get rid of that smell.*

It wasn't the oinking that led him to the sty; it was the goddam stink. The occupant was a huge sow with a bunch of noisily sucking piglets.

What to do? Larry opened the gate, grabbed the closest little porky, and ran toward the cornfield. He figured the sow would follow him, and the piglets would follow their mamma. He wheeled around, stopping in a clearing. The squealing of the baby was driving him nuts. He strangled the thing and threw it on the ground. Momma couldn't stop in time. She crashed into her little one, crushing it into the dirt with her sharp hooves and enormous weight. She glared at Larry and squealed in rage.

Larry hauled the gun out of his belt, aimed, and pulled the trigger. The sow was finally quiet. The babies hid in the rows of corn, trembling in fear. *Hey, the buggers can take care of themselves.*

As he walked back to the house, a broad smile blossomed on his gaunt face. *Yeah, I'll go to that Quicky-Save and get me some food. Mmm, bacon. That'll be good.*

Suddenly, he tripped, landing hard on the dead piglet. Its sharp little hoof dug into his cheek. He lay there dazed and confused. He left the damned carcass back in the clearing. *How did it get here? When dead pigs fly, right?*

Swiping at the blood dripping from his chin, Larry stood up on shaky legs. He fell again near the house, narrowly missing impaling himself on an upturned pitchfork. On the soft ground, he saw hoof prints. Lots of pig prints. Some were even bigger than the sow's. The old man had said watch out for the pigs, plural. *Nah, there was only one. Little piggies don't count, right?*

Getting up more slowly, he threw the pitchfork into the empty sty. *Damn, now I hear oinking.* It grew louder, angrier, nearer. He turned around looking for the source.

The pitchfork vibrated, then lifted from the muck. It rotated at an agonizingly slow pace, drawing out his horror. It hung in the air as three pigs rose up out of the dirt.

A big boar, the fat, bloody sow, and the squashed piglet.

Larry squealed as the pitchfork picked up speed as the trio raced towards him. A weird thought passed through his mind as the sharp, mucky implement struck home. It was his last thought. *Goddam Porkergeists.*

Shadows of the Dark Moon

Leonard Little

THE SKY WEEPS IN bitter sorrow as I peer through a window in time, seeing demons, like shadows of the dark moon, their yellow eyes gleaming as they creep from the thorns.

The window clouds with misty air that whirls and eddies all around me. I find myself in the body of a young boy, pelting from the house, arms churning for greater speed. I cross a bridge and look upstream at more demon eyes—a whole pack glaring hungrily from the banks. Their eyes follow me as I continue my course, but they dare not give chase. And I know why.

Candlelight shines through the window of my destination and I see my friend, a guardian, black as the night, running beside me, matching my every jump and stride with his quick feet.

My friend snarls and the demons ahead slink low, hissing dark wraths, as they flee back into the thorns, allowing me passage.

Mist covers time's window again as days flicker past, then seasons. I grow taller, stronger, bolder. I construct a fort in the fallow field between the village and the thorns so I can thwart the demons who dare to venture from their hidden lairs. Sunup to sundown, my guardian and I keep vigil at the fort's turret.

Again, Mist covers the window and clears. My guardian is waking me with a call to arms. I leap to my feet and rush to the turret, but my fearless guardian darts from the fort. I follow reluctantly, my feet dragging in fear as sunlight fades to darkness.

A dragon roars from the highway sending icy rivulets

through my marrow. My feet quicken, but my guardian is faster, disappearing into the night. As I crest a final hill I see him in the fiery gaze of a silver dragon that thunders past him, leaving a trail of blue smoke swirling into the night sky.

A solitary yelp stops me cold.

When the smoke finally clears, all that is left is the broken body of my best friend. I stumble to the road and fall beside him, weeping as I stroke his cooling fur.

As the morning sun breaks over the horizon I lift his small stiff body from the road and take him back to our fort.

The rain quickens, falling like tears as I force a shovel deep into the earth. At first, I dig slowly with purpose, but guilt and anger give power to my efforts. My hair gets soaked. My cheeks turn red, burning with the cold of the day. I soon have a grave, deep and wide enough to be my own. I climb out and wrap a small black spaniel in a blanket from his bed and I lay him to rest.

Retrieving the shovel, I look around, watching as the scene before me melts with change. The stout walls of my fort become a rusted old Buick with warped plywood form-ing the upper deck. The turret is an old wringer washing machine and feral cats, not demons, dart in and out of the blackberry vines along the banks of an irrigation ditch near my house. I cover my friend with dirt and kneel beside the freshly covered grave, then I look up and see an old man peering through the window of time.

I roll my wheelchair back from the window, and my eyes clinch shut, as new tears stream down my weathered face. I feel the old wound of grief reopen in my heart, turning loose the pain I'd locked deep in my soul for forty years. I still missed my truest friend. I missed the adventures we took through a world filled with demons and forts. I missed his warm breath next to me while I slept, but most of all I missed the boy that I was back when my friend and guardian was alive. A boy that could run like the wind and go on adventures with his best friend.

Turning my back to the window, I dry my eyes and roll down the hallway to my study. There on my desk, a computer screen glares back, its window is as misty and blank as the widow in time. I set my fingers to the keys and mist clears. I realize at that moment, I hadn't lost anything. The worlds of my imagination wait patiently beneath my fingertips. Waiting for each keystroke to reveal the next challenge. My guardian and truest friend is alive within my heart. His courage drives the heroes to new heights of bravery in the pages of my stories. The boy that I remember is there too, he faces demons, dragons, and monsters, pitting the magic of love and truth against the forces of evil that threaten his world.

About the Contributors

FRANK BARRERA writes and illustrates his own books for children. He has shown his sculptures and paintings in galleries around California for the past 25 years. He continues to create new worlds of fantasy for children of all ages.

CHRIS CROWE started out in life to be a stand up comic, but found out he could make more money as a student teacher. After 40 years in the classroom he still enjoys teaching and working with students. He has had the opportunity to teach the children of his former students and hopes to be around to teach their grandchildren. Chris got married a few months after his eighteenth birthday. After almost 50 years, five children, and ten grandchildren he is still in love with his lovely bride, Judy, and is a devoted father and grandfather. He started writing stories to entertain his children and many of his stories feature his children as protagonists. As life often brings encounters with selfish, unkind people, his antagonists are often former bosses, principals, or associates. While names are changed to prevent the guilty from taking him to court, it is not unlikely they would recognize themselves. Chris likes to write fantasy Sci-fi for the young adult and likes to see his name in print as Dr. C.H. Crowe. He earned the degree and the sound of "Doctor" makes him smile.

LEE GARRETT: An identical twin, Lee Garrett was born in Selena, Missouri, and raised in Fort Smith, Arkansas. He attended Westark Community College, majoring in Bible and Social Sciences before transferring to Missouri Baptist College in Saint Louis. He served in the Navy as a Religious Program Specialist with the Chaplain's Corps and made two Mediterranean/Indian Ocean cruises. He later drifted across the south and southwest, spending twenty years out in California before following his muse on again. He pursued music expression through local coffeehouses as a singer/songwriter, and performed concerts for local churches. Lee currently resides in Corpus Christi, Texas. Devoted to the Renaissance Ideal of well-versed diversity, Lee plays piano, guitar, Native American ghost flute, writes fiction, lyric poetry, music composition, paints, draws, and is knowledgeable in the fields of theoretical physics, world cultures, and philosophy. After mastering five styles of Gung-Fu, he has created an integrated martial arts style with the efficiency of a non-classical approach and the classic beauty of the Shou-lin arts, merging both, producing a "Full Circle" path".

DENNIS GRAYSON has 40 years of experience as a television Writer/Producer/Director. In Sacramento, CA he worked at KCRA-TV, KRBK-TV and KQCA-TV. Other markets include: Dayton, Cincinnati, and Los Angeles.

Out of over 20 screenplays he has written, 4 were sold and 3 were produced and distributed, making profits for the producers. He also Unit Production Managed 4 films and 2nd Unit Directed 3 films.

He is a Past-President of California Writers Club.

Dennis recently completed his fourth novel. Two of these, *Braca* and *End Times*, are self-published and are available at Kindle and Amazon Prime. Currently, he has turned his attention to short stories, two of which are included in this anthology.

LEO LITTLE: Imagination and fantasy came early to Leonard as he sat at his grandfather's knees and listened to the wonderful tales of rabbits and a family of berries. Both his grandfathers were great storytellers, his grandmother wrote a book of poems and his father published a book based on the Bible. To this great tradition, Leonard is happy to add his own stories.

Born in November of 1963, he lives now in the city of his birth Sacramento, CA. He is a father, grandfather, husband and son. He loves his family and hopes to hear their laughter throughout his life.

He has worked as a landscaper and then a truck driver, before an accident at work left him disabled. He has since taken up writing and has met with writers from two critique groups: The Warped Spacers and SMOG. The wonderful people in both groups have helped him craft his fantasies into stories that will hopefully touch the hearts and souls of his readers.

JUDY PREY: After working for over forty years as a physical therapist, Judy retired and now has the time to feed her passions. Writing, volunteering at Sutter's Fort, and creating beaded jewelry for sale at craft shows are just some of her interests. Discovering new avenues for adventure keeps the brain happy and healthy, she says.

STEVE PREY is a retired State engineer who has a keen interest in the technologies of the universe and understanding how all the parts fit together. He looks for patterns as to where life and its related tech is heading. He has two books under development, provides illustrations for fellow authors, and reviews group submissions. Delving into the world of speculative fiction is creative fun. He uses the same skill sets to assist various committees and task forces of the National Academies of Science to explore and develop creative solutions to the world's changing climate. These challenges impact our future readers' lives.

AMY ROGERS earned a bunch of advanced degrees in science and medicine but threw it all away to write science-themed fiction. Learn more at AmyRogers.com about the microbes and mayhem in her page-turning science thriller novels described as "frighteningly realistic", "superb", and "gripping" by #1 *NYT* bestselling author James Rollins, *SF Book Review*, and *Foreword Reviews*.

CAROLINE WILLIAMS has led an eclectic life that began with her decision to enlist in the Navy forty-eight years ago. She participated in several historical reenactment groups and earned a BA degree in history. She was and still is an avid reader of science fiction, fantasy and mystery novels. For several years Caroline worked in the public sector and in her spare time critiqued manuscripts as a member of the Warped Spacers. Caroline currently lives in Sacramento, California with her cat Tesseract and has started her writing career.

Caroline extends a special thank you to Scott Wiggers, Apau Hawaii Tours, who documented the Kilauea eruption from start to finish and for his help on questions concerning the eruption. She also thanks the Hawaiian community for allowing the world access to their myths and legends especially the legend of Pele.

Finally thanks to Shari Griffin, Judy Prey, and the group she affectionately calls The Crew for their support and suggestions while she was writing this story.

In memoriam

Kathleen L'Ecluse,
Dave Murray,
and
Scott Smith

who have gone on to other worlds.

Made in the USA
Middletown, DE
03 December 2022

16642597R00123